PUZZLES

BOOK 2

A Detective Love Story

Russell F. Moran

Puzzles – Book Two
A Detective Love Story

Coddington Press

Copyright © 2019 by Russell F. Moran

www.morancom.com

Printed in the United States of America

ISBN-978-1-7338872-2-9

Covers and text design by LuAnn T. Palazzo
www.TheDesignDiva.net

DEDICATION

This book is dedicated to the men and women police detectives.

ACKNOWLEDGEMENTS

As always, I thank my wife, Lynda, for her attentive reading, rereading, and editing of my many drafts, and for laughing at my jokes. Lynda is to me as Bobbie is to Bob. I also thank my friend and editor, John White, for his keen editorial eye. I thank LuAnn T. Palazzo for her expert interior and cover designs. I also thank Dennis Ciano, retired NYPD homicide detective, for his expert advice. And I especially thank my readers, many of whom are a constant source of inspiration and encouragement for me.

AUTHOR'S NOTE

Puzzles Book 2 is the second book of *The Puzzles Series*, the adventures of detectives Bob and Bobbie. Bob and Bobbie are two of my favorite characters, and I think of them as old friends. As I wrote this book, we took a lot of adventures together. I hope you will see them that way too.

You will find a **Cast of Characters** after the last chapter of the book. It can be frustrating to come across a character on page 150, that you first met on page 20, especially if you've put the book down for a few days. I've seen this done in Russian literature, and I happily add a cast of characters to *Puzzles* as well as my other novels.

CHAPTER 1

Bobbie

That big tall handsome guy was here to see me this morning. I think he was, or maybe I'm dreaming. I only saw him once briefly, when I was able to peel my eyes open for a couple of moments. I just wish I could remember his name. Shit, I wish I could remember my own name. Does he really exist, or is he somebody I wished would exist? The guy's movie-star handsome, or at least he was in my dream. I feel like I'm in some sort of cocoon I've read about in science fiction novels, stories about people abducted by aliens and held against their will, encased in an object from which they can't escape.

I can feel the sheets beneath me, I can feel an occasional breeze, but mostly I feel the pounding pain in my head. It's relentless. I can hear people talking, sometimes too loud. I think they're in a hallway outside of the room I'm in. I try to open my eyes again.

Won't happen. It's as if they're glued shut. I see that guy again, or I am I dreaming that I'm see him again? Yes, I definitely recall seeing him, or hearing him. I think he said his name is Bud, or Rob, or maybe Bob. This isn't working. I find that thinking is like trying to mix heavy cement with a cookie dough mixer.

I have no idea where I am or how I got here. Hell, I have no idea *who* I am. I'm just lying inside my cocoon, a cocoon that includes a throbbing headache. Wait, it's coming back to me. I'm 10 years old and I live in New York City, in the Whitestone section of Queens, I think. I'm on my tricycle and riding up and down my parents' driveway, which is 15 feet wide, a house on either side. It just stopped raining and the sun came out. Our little cocker spaniel, Puddles, is licking at my ankles. We call him Puddles because that's what he constantly leaves around the house. My mom calls. "Hey, honey, wake up." But I *am* awake, I'm riding my tricycle, and I can see Puddles next to me. I can see him, but I can't hear him. Maybe he doesn't like to bark. I hear Mom calling again, but I can't answer her. This fucking cocoon is getting old, real old.

I feel a soft, gentle hand squeeze mine. "Here, Detective, have some more water. You're not taking in enough liquids."

Detective? Is that my name? But I thought that big handsome guy was named Detective. Shit, I'd be happy to get through a simple thought without going blank again. The soft hand reaches behind my neck and gently moves my head forward, putting a glass of water next to my lips. It tastes good, but then I start coughing, making my head feel as if it were about to explode. Then I fall asleep again, which is a good thing. My dreams sure beat the hell out this strange reality.

I'm sitting at a pretty restaurant on the Chicago River having lunch with a tall influential-looking man. The place looks really familiar. I live in Chicago, I think, or am I dreaming that? The guy— of course I can't remember his name—seems intent on something. He keeps

2

leaning forward while he talks to me. I have no idea what he said, but he seemed to take it quite seriously. I do recall him inviting me to visit him in New York at the New York Police Department. Why? Am I in some sort of trouble?

Wait—I think I took a job with the NYPD as it's called. I remember my first day. Yes, I definitely remember that. Maybe my mental cobwebs are starting to clear a bit. I walk into an office and there he is, that tall, handsome man I keep dreaming about. I remember his eyes, the most beautiful eyes I ever saw. I don't recall the name of the color, but I think it's faizel, no hazel. He seems to be friendly and polite, but I have no idea what he was doing there. Mr. Handsome keeps calling me partner, whatever that means. He smiles a lot, which is great because he has a beautiful smile, the most gorgeous smile I've ever seen. The dream stops, and I go blank again.

Now I'm walking into an office. That tall good-looking guy is naked and a beautiful brunette with long legs is under him on the desk, also naked. Her name is Monica Gordon. I don't know how I know her name. They're going at it heavily. I clear my throat, and they both look at me, smile and wave. I don't wave back. Nor do I smile.

In the morning, my eyes open a bit. I think it's morning because the sun is shining through the window. During the night I recall having some bad dreams, but fortunately I can't remember them, not all of them anyway.

I'm standing in the middle of a large living room. Two people, a man and a woman, are lying near me in a pool of blood. They're not moving, and I think they're dead. I'm holding a gun, a Sig Sauer 226 pistol. Am I a cop or something? I know I didn't shoot them because my gun is cold. I'm standing over a bright pink bassinet looking at the most adorable little girl I've ever seen. She's around two years old I figure, a gorgeous little blond bundle. She's crying gently, and I bend over her to see if she's okay. I take a photo of her with my phone. That's when I hear a shot from behind me, the loudest shot I've ever heard. That's the last thing I remember, besides that beautiful little girl in the bassinette.

A nurse walks into the room carrying yet another pitcher of water. "Hi Lauren," I hear myself say.

"Oh my God, you remembered my name. Your memory is definitely coming back," Lauren says. "Do you know where you are?"

"Well, a hospital of some sort, I think. But why am I here?"

"Because, Detective, you were shot in the head at the base of your skull. We've been worried about you, really worried," Lauren said. "But your doctor said he doesn't think you've suffered any permanent brain damage."

"Detective?"

"Yes, you're the famous detective Bobbie Nelson."

I close my eyes and I'm sleeping again. The dream comes back to me, in vivid color. I'm standing over that adorable little girl, wanting more than anything in my life to help her, to console her, to stop her from crying. Her parents are lying not four feet away in a pool of blood. I'm holding a gun. Then comes the loud sound.

I open my eyes and Lauren is standing there. I'm seeing a lot clearer now, and my head doesn't hurt nearly as much as it did a short time ago.

"You just had another one of your terrible dreams, honey. Don't worry. They'll go away in time."

"My memories are starting to come back to me, Lauren. Shit, that dream about me standing over that gorgeous little girl isn't a dream. It really happened. I was looking at her when everything went blank.

Do you know where the little girl is?"

"She's with Child Protective Services. I know those folks and they're good people. They'll take excellent care of her until they can find a foster home. Both her parents were killed by the same man who shot you."

A foster home?

"How long have I been here, Lauren?"

"Six weeks, Bobbie. Six long weeks. Hey, there's a special visitor here to see you."

CHAPTER 2

Bobbie

I dozed off again. When I open my eyes, that tall handsome guy I keep dreaming about is standing there, the guy who I caught screwing that gorgeous brunette, Monica Gordon.

He reaches out and grabs my hand. Something about his grip feels familiar. Then he leans over and kisses me. Oh, my God, what a wonderful kiss. It was soft and gentle, but at the same time excited, wanting, imploring. And that cologne, I know the smell of that cologne. I definitely know that smell. I can almost *feel* the scent of that cologne. I close my eyes and the scent of the cologne inhabits not just my lungs but my entire body.

"I don't think your friend, Monica, would like to see you kiss me like that," I hear myself saying.

He looks confused.

"Monica? Monica who?" Mr. Handsome says.

"Monica Gordon," I say. "The last time I saw her, you two were naked and really going at it on top of a desk. I think it was *my* desk."

Mr. Handsome cracks up in hysterical laughter.

"You're acting like you don't know her," I say. I don't know why I'm being bitchy about this. If this handsome stranger wants to screw a beautiful woman, who am I to say no? But in my dreams, I've taken a liking to this guy—a *real* liking, so I guess that's why I feel insanely jealous about him screwing that babe.

"Yes," he says, still laughing, "I know Monica Gordon quite well, and so do you. She works at Child Protective Services. She's their oldest employee at 88 years of age."

Now I'm confused. That chick I saw him screwing was definitely not 88 years old. Was I dreaming? Again?

"Do you mind if I ask who you are?" I say, still angry with my bizarre jealousy over this handsome stranger humping a beautiful woman on my desk.

He leans over and puts his face next to mine. Oh, my God, that cologne again. I know it from somewhere. Yes, I know it. Memories start flooding into my mind. I take a deep breath.

"I'm your husband, baby, Bob Lawton."

My memories start to stack up like they're falling out of the sky. My husband? Yes, all of a sudden, my brain is full of him, every inch of him, every moment with him. His gorgeous face, his amazing eyes, his sleek muscular body. I love this guy.

"I could sure use another kiss," I say.

He leans into my face and smothers me with those gorgeous lips. I close my eyes. I know those lips; I know them better than my own body. I *own* those lips. He begins to pull his head back.

"No, please don't stop. I want the feel of your lips."

"I've missed you, baby," he says. "I love you."

"You love me? I love you, Bob. Oh my God, do I love you."

I circled my arms around his neck and never wanted to let go. Was he really screwing that hot brunette on my desk? Maybe not, but it sure seems real. Maybe I was imagining him screwing *me*.

He stood and stroked my face as he took off his jacket. Strange how some things wrap around my heart. The act of taking off his jacket told me he wants to stay—with *me*. It's like he was making a statement by taking off his jacket. An old phrase just popped into my head—a dream come true?

Two days later Bob was again standing next to my bed when I woke up. My God is this man handsome. And he's my husband! He stroked my face. I love when he does that.

"When am I getting out of here?"

He squeezed my hand. "Your doctor says you're good to go today. I've arranged for a private duty nurse and I'm also taking some vacation days, so I'll be with you. We have a lot of catching up to do. Hey, do you remember where we live?"

"Yeah, 25 Park Row, just three blocks from One Police Plaza. We just renovated it a few months ago."

"How about our vacation home?"

"Oh, yes," I say, "our gorgeous house in East Hampton. I love skinny dipping in our huge pool and screwing nonstop in the hot tub." I am totally not dreaming this.

"I think it's safe to say that your amnesia is officially behind you,

Bobbie. Let's get you ready to go home."

CHAPTER 3

Bobbie

B ob and I got to our apartment at 4:30 in the afternoon. Although I've been in a semi coma for the past six weeks, I feel like I've missed the place. When the next-door tenant moved out last year, we tore down the wall and turned our 1,500 square foot apartment into a 3,000 square foot beauty. It felt great to be home. It was precisely as I recalled it. Precisely. My brain has definitely become unscrambled. Today is our second wedding anniversary, and we planned to celebrate later at our favorite French restaurant, La Grenouille on 52nd Street. Beats the shit out of a coma.

I was tired as hell, so I decided to take a nap before our celebration. The doctor told me I should expect to feel fatigue for a couple of weeks. Immediately I became lost in reverie—about the amazing past two years. Sometimes your mind goes to where it wants to go, even if you're trying to take a nap. My neurosurgeon told me it's a good idea to review memories, so I did. All my life I've been blessed with eidetic imagery or a photographic memory. I'm happy to say it's all coming back. The scent of Bob's cologne helps.

Sometimes you get lucky, I thought.

I'm a cop, a 37-year-old Detective First Grade with the NYPD to be specific. I'm not supposed to believe in luck with my work. My job is to pour over the evidence, interrogate people, look for clues, and put it all together. My job is to solve puzzles. Luck has nothing to do with it.

Bullshit. I'm the luckiest cop in the world. I say that for one reason, and the reason is a man named Bob Lawton. He's my husband, my detective partner, and my lover. He's also my best friend. Bob saved my life. After I was shot, Bob came running into the room and fired at the guy who shot me, killing him before he could get off another round.

Two and a half years ago, I was a detective with the Chicago Police Department. One day, a day I will never forget, I got a call from a famous guy named Ralph Norquist, Commissioner of the New York Police Department. He said he'd like to fly out to Chicago and have lunch with me. Lunch? With me? I recall dreaming about that meeting when I was in the hospital. But it really did happen. My brain is regaining its ability to distinguish dreams from real memories.

The commissioner and I planned to have lunch at the River Roast restaurant on North LaSalle Street overlooking the Chicago River. The place advertises itself as a new American spin on British food, served in an upscale restaurant. It was his suggestion. I thought that was a bit strange given that I lived in Chicago, and it would seem appropriate for me to pick the lunch spot. But what was I going to do, argue with a famous, powerful guy?

It was a mild sunny day in May, so the commissioner and I sat at an outside table right on the Chicago River. Ever since I lived in Chicago, I found that looking at the gentle, meandering river always calms me down, which was a good thing because I was nervous as hell. Ralph, as he insisted I call him, told me he'd heard and read about my detective skills. He's a tall, good-looking man at 6'2," impeccably dressed, with deep brown eyes. He has black hair streaked with hints of gray. I read that he was 57 years old, married and had one son in college. That would make him 59 or 60 years-old today. I have a habit of doing research before a meeting, a good practice for a detective. I recalled that he had a way of looking at me that I found intimidating. But that's okay; I'm easily intimidated, especially around powerful people.

A colleague of mine, Mike Toner, a Chicago detective and an old friend of Ralph's, had told him about me.

"Mike tells me you're the best detective he's ever worked with, and he's been around for a while. So, I Googled your name and wow, the world of journalism seems fascinated with your work, not to mention your good looks. That big *Johnston* multiple murder case seemed like it was a closed file until you took over. The reporter who wrote the article in the *Chicago Tribune* was blown away by your scientific approach to your job. A five-year-old case involving seven dead bodies, and you opened it up and nailed the perps by reworking the forensic evidence. The reporter referred to you as a "real life Sherlock Holmes."

I guess I should have felt like hot stuff being interviewed by the renowned Ralph Norquist. There was a lot of talk that the president may nominate him for attorney general. I chose to ignore his comment about my "good looks." Why do powerful guys think it's necessary to flirt when they want to make a point?

I'm a bit skilled at interpreting non-verbal language clues, and Norquist seemed to want to do some heavy persuading. He kept leaning so far forward (a sure sign of someone wanting to connect) that I thought his face would fall into his soup. Obviously, he wants to make me an offer of some sort. Or maybe he's writing a book and just wants to use me for background. Self-doubt to the rescue. I have a big problem in my life—I struggle with self-doubt. I suppose I should feel nothing but self-confidence, but it never seems to work out that way. I have a stupid habit of expecting the worst. I graduated from the University of Chicago Law School, one of the best in the country. Of course, I didn't expect to be accepted when I applied, my self-doubt trying to save me from disappointment. I had good grades as an undergraduate at Yale and I scored well on the law school admission test, but my self-doubt never let up.

Turns out, my self-doubt was wasted. Not only was I accepted on the first round, but I was awarded a full academic scholarship.

I put my self-doubt on hold, and tried to enjoy my lunch, with my stomach in a fucking knot. But my gut and his facial signals told me he wanted to make me a job offer.

"Bobbie, I'm sure you've heard about the problems the NYPD is going through, the biggest corruption scandal on record. Not only have we found hundreds of crooked cops, but the unions themselves are also corrupt to the core. That's why, on direct orders from the mayor and the city council, I've begun recruiting cops, especially detectives, from other police departments. You've got one hell of a background, Bobbie. You're a cop but you graduated from one of the best law schools in the country. In a way you remind me of that Jamie character on *Blue Bloods,* my favorite show. In the show, young Jamie graduated from Harvard Law School but chose to follow the family tradition and become a cop. But you're different. First, obviously you're a woman, a very pretty one at that, (*there he goes again*) and second, you're a senior detective not a uniformed officer. And you're only 35 years old."

I try to ignore flattery, but this guy knew how to do it. I was beginning to feel like serious hot shit.

"Bobbie, I want you to come and work for the NYPD, the best police department in the country, or at least it was until this goddam scandal hit. I offer you a job as a Detective First Grade. My research tells me that you make $80,000 with the Chicago Police Department. One of our detectives at your level earned $160,000 last year including overtime. An old friend of mine (this guy seemed to have a lot of 'old friends') is the publisher of the *New York Daily News*. He wants you, the famous Bobbie Nelson, to write a weekly column on police matters. I know you love to write, having read a few of your articles in the Chicago PD newsletter. For that part-time job with the *Daily News* you will be paid $45,000 a year. So, you can make over $200,000 a year, including the writing gig. With your background you can probably knock out an article every week in two hours. I know that you're single, having divorced two years ago, and have little family in the Chicago area. Hell, you grew up in New York City, so you won't have a lot of adjusting to do. Bobbie, with your brains and skills you deserve the limelight of the best police department in the country. It will do wonders for your career. I don't doubt that someday you may occupy my chair as commissioner (As I said, this guy is quite skilled at flattery). Please accept my offer to at least come to New York and check us out in more detail. No pressure. You can make your final decision after you visit us in New York."

The rest is history. I took him up on his offer for me to visit the NYPD before making my final decision. Truth is, I was ready to sign before we finished lunch in Chicago. So, I flew to New York, was given a tour of the NYPD, and accepted the job. I reported for duty a month later—the luckiest day of my life. I say that because I got to meet my partner, Detective First Grade Bob Lawton, the man who inhabited my dreams while I was in the hospital. I had seen pictures of him, and I knew that he was cute as hell, but when I met him in person, my heart skipped a beat. I thought he was the handsomest man I had ever seen, and still do. Bob is my age, 37, and tall at 6'3". He has light sandy brown hair, heavenly hazel-colored eyes, and a muscular athletic build that always takes my breath away. I tried to ignore his physical attractiveness, recalling that my ex-husband was also quite good-looking. But he turned out to be a wife-beating drunk; hence my divorce.

Like Bob, I work out regularly, and, I must admit, I have the body to show for it. I'm told that I'm not hard to look at, and from the first day we met, I noticed Bob noticing. He didn't look at me with leering eyes, however, but politely complimented me on my figure. Bob is a gentleman.

From our first day on the job together, Bob and I threw ourselves into the cases the commissioner assigned to us. Commissioner Norquist discovered, within a few days, that he could assign the toughest cases to Bob and me, and we'd get the job done. I consider myself an excellent detective, and I was happy to see that my new partner was a complete pro.

Besides working our cases, we also began to be attracted to each other—*really attracted*. After a particularly trying day, Bob and I had dinner—a date really. We had been partnered for just over a month. By that time, I realized that I was no longer just attracted to him; I was drop-dead, crazy in love with him. I'll never forget reaching out and grabbing his hand, all the while staring into those gorgeous hazel eyes. I told him that I loved him. I was nervous as hell that I was going forward too fast. He stood and pulled his chair next to mine, put his big strong arm around me, and gave me the most exciting kiss of my life. He first brushed his lips over mine, teasing me. Then he pushed forward, enveloping my mouth, driving me totally crazy. His kiss said it all—I was his, and he was mine.

We finished our light dinner. We weren't really hungry, for food anyway, and went to Bob's apartment right nearby. After slowly disrobing each other, we showered and made love, the most fantastic love I could ever imagine, and I have a good imagination. I stroked his muscular back as he entered me. He gently went in and out, slowly at first, then thrusting hard and fast, bringing me to an earth-shattering climax at the same time as he came. I will never forget that orgasm. And the great thing is that Bob brings me back to that wonderful place often—*very* often. Soon after that, Bob proposed marriage, and we tied the knot a month later.

Yes, I'm the luckiest cop in the world.

So, I didn't get much of a nap, but I did luxuriate in my wonderful memories of when Bob and I first met. I rolled over and noticed that Bob was lying next to me, breathing softly, wearing a big smile. I reached over, stroked his face, and deeply inhaled the scent of his cologne. My God, do I love this man. I don't have to think about it, I can feel it. It's like my love for him inhabits every pore of my body.

CHAPTER 4

Bob

I don't think Bobbie got much of her well-needed nap. She took a lot of deep breaths. I noticed her smiling constantly and chuckling often. I've taken off a few days so I can assume grandmother duty and watch over her. I still have a hard time coping with her having been shot. She almost lost her life, and with it, my life. I sure need some sleep, but my mind keeps wandering backward.

Bobbie has a wonderful habit of saying sweet things. The day we married, she told me she's the luckiest cop in the world. Although we seldom disagree, I told her that I didn't agree. *I'm* the luckiest cop in the world.

A couple of weeks later she said another sweet thing I'll never forget.

"Hey, Bob, you're my lover, my partner, and my husband. But you're also my best friend. I don't just love you, I *like* you."

I understand what she means, and I feel the same way. When you *like* your partner, you enjoy working together, you complete each other's sentences, do little favors for each other, and just enjoy being together. I do think I'm the luckiest cop in the world.

I have a hard time believing that just a couple of years ago, I was worried as hell about my new partner, and we hadn't even met in person yet. When the commissioner told me who I'd be partnered with after my current partner retired, I was almost sick to my stomach. Bobbie Nelson was probably the most famous detective in the country. Newspaper and magazine articles constantly mentioned her, along with photos of her stunningly beautiful face. She was also on TV regularly being interviewed about one of her cases. Given her fame, I had the sinking feeling that I was about to be partnered with an insufferable obnoxious bitch, a scene-stealing princess who didn't care for the opinion of others.

I was wrong. After our first day on the job together, I realized that she was not only a hell of a good detective, but she was also sweet and polite, not to mention impossibly gorgeous. When I think of Bobbie's physical appearance, I envision three vectors of feminine attractiveness converging on her. She's beautiful, cute, and pretty, usually all at the same time. By the end of that first day, I realized that I liked my new partner—*a lot.*

I will never forget that dinner date after we worked together for a month. Bobbie, who doesn't suffer from shyness, reached out, grabbed my hand across the table, looked into my eyes and said she loved me. I pulled my chair next to hers, put my arm around her and kissed her. Then I told her that I loved her. That was just over two years ago. I love her more now than I did then. I love her more every day that goes by. Whatever shit comes downhill, my love for Bobbie sustains me. During the past six weeks, as Bobbie was recovering in the hospital, I thought I'd lose my mind. Not being able to communicate with her in her semi-comatose state was one of the worst times in my life. But now she's on the mend, almost completely her old self, and I'm lying next to her in bed. Did

I mention how lucky I am?

I rolled over after getting a few moments of a nap. I looked at Bobbie lying next to me. She wore a big smile on her face. She's all mine—and I'm hers. She leaned over and kissed me.

"Did you get much of your well-needed nap?" I asked.

"I didn't nap much, but I had a great time with some wonderful memories."

"Memories about what?"

"Memories of you, baby. Gimme another kiss."

"Hey, honey, we have reservations at our favorite restaurant. We should get ready and go to our anniversary celebration."

"I think we should start our celebration right here. We can change our reservation to later. The doctor said I should start to get regular exercise, and I don't need to tell you what's my favorite exercise. Make love to me, Bob. Make me crazy as only you can do. Bring me to that wonderful mountaintop. Why don't you help me out of my clothes and join me in the shower?"

I think we both put our nap time to good use. Having Bobbie back in my arms makes life worth living.

CHAPTER 5

Bobbie

Bob and I make love a lot—*A lot.* But there was something about our second wedding anniversary celebration last night that was beyond special. We skipped our dinner at La Grenouille, and opted instead for occasional snacks of soft frozen vanilla yogurt, our favorite post-sex indulgence. And, wow, did we ever do a lot of indulging last night. I'm pretty good with numbers, but I can't count how many times we made love. My Bob has amazing stamina—simply amazing. Nice to be out of the hospital.

The next day we walked to our favorite diner for breakfast. Some habits never change, and this is one of them. The diner is four blocks from our apartment, and three blocks from One Police Plaza (aka One PP). I was still on sick leave for the next couple of weeks so we wouldn't be heading for the office. When we got back to the apartment, I decided I'd tell Bob all about my dreams while I was in the hospital, including the crazy one about me catching him screwing a foxy brunette on my desk. We still laugh about that, but the dream seemed so vivid, my stomach goes into a knot when I recall it.

But one dream never leaves me, the one about me standing over that adorable little girl with her parents lying dead a few feet away, right before I was shot. I still see that little girl in my mind. Well, it wasn't a dream; it really happened. I started to cry. Bob, sitting next to me on the couch, put his arms around me. He's my rock, my boulder, one I can always count on to steady me.

"Tell me about her," Bob said.

"She's two years old, with blond hair and the cutest little face I've ever seen. It broke my heart to see her crying. I called Child Protective Services yesterday and she's still there, waiting until they find a foster home. I can't get her adorable face out of my mind."

I showed Bob a photo I snapped with my phone just before I was shot. From the look on his face, I could see his heart melting. He had seen her too that day, but being reminded brought his heart to his throat.

"She needs a loving new family," Bob said, as he squeezed my knee.

"Oh yes," I said, tears running down my face, "oh my God does she ever need a loving family."

Bob leaned over, put his arm around me, and kissed me on the neck.

"So, let's give her one," Bob said.

"What?" I grabbed Bob's face in both my hands and stared into his eyes. "Please repeat what you just said, baby."

"Let's give that beautiful little girl a loving home. I can't think of a more loving home than ours. Let's adopt her, honey."

I sat on his lap, wrapped my arms around his neck, and kissed him. Then I kissed him again.

"Oh, my God, whatever I did to deserve you, baby, I want to keep on doing it. I love you, Bob. I'm crazy in love with you."

———————

I immediately called Child Protective Services, an agency that Bob and I sadly deal with often as detectives. But there was nothing sad about this call. Bob then called Commissioner Ralph and asked him to put in a good word for us. The agency is quite careful about finding a foster home for an orphan, and they should be. Those people are dedicated to making life better for kids, kids who are suddenly thrust into a strange and scary new reality. I called and made an appointment for the following morning. We went to the medical department to get copies of our latest physicals and blood tests, which we knew would be required. I was so excited I thought my heart would pound out of my chest.

Bob and I were about to be interviewed by Dolores Clemente, the executive director of Child Protective Services, a woman who knows us well. We sat in the waiting room. Old Monica Gordon strolled by using her walker. Monica Gordon, the name of the woman I dreamed I saw Bob screwing. She smiled and greeted us.

"Why don't you wait here while I go get me a little action," Bob said.

"Okay, wiseass, no more jokes about my hospital dreams," I said, laughing.

Dolores walked into the room to greet us and we followed her into her office. Dolores is tall and business-like, with a personality that says don't give me any bullshit. She's well-known for taking a personal interest in the kids under her care. She gestured for us to sit in the chairs facing her desk.

"One concern I have is that you both have full time occupations. Who will take care of the little girl when you're both at work?"

Then I pointed out to her that our apartment is three blocks from Police Plaza, and one of us can run home on a moment's notice. What nailed it for her was our financial status. We have money coming out of our ears, from Bob's inheritance, our huge book royalties, and our combined salaries, more than enough to hire help as needed. Dolores smiled and nodded her head when I said that.

"I've seen you both many times and how you treat the kids you have to bring here. You two may be cops, but around kids you're the gentlest cops I've ever encountered. I'm not going to slow things down by taking this to the board, so I'm making an executive decision. You're officially approved. That little bundle is all yours."

I thought I'd faint.

"What's her name?" Bob asked.

"Tillary. Her late parents had a law practice on Tillary Street in Brooklyn, and I guess that's how she got her name."

I decided to ask the big question.

"When can we take her home, Dolores?"

"We have your medical records and blood tests and you've filled out all the paperwork, so she's good to go right now. I think she's been here long enough."

"Let's go!" I said, probably too loud.

Dolores walked us to the nursery. Little Tillary was sitting on the floor playing with another child. She looked just as cute as I saw her in my memories. I walked over to her and said "Hi."

Oh my God, I must be imagining this I thought. She looked up at me with a wide smile and a look of recognition on her face, as if she recalled seeing me before. *Before* I got shot in the head that is. Logic tells me that she can't possibly remember me. But screw it. Sometimes logic needs to take a second seat to happy emotions. I will always keep in my mind and heart the expression on little Tillary's face at that moment.

Bob scooped her up in his arms and we left for Tillary's new home, her new loving home. Bob and I decided to give Tillary a nickname—*Tilly*.

CHAPTER 6

Bobbie

I think I know Bob better than I know any other human being, but what I never knew was how wonderful he is around kids—our kid, our daughter, our Tilly. As we walked up to our apartment door, I noticed that the hallway was lined with boxes. Unbeknownst to me, last night Bob had called the local toy store and bought 25 cuddly toys. He handed her to me as he started to gather up the boxes to bring to Tilly's room. As I put together lunch, Bob was down on all fours, showing Tilly her new toys. He talked nonstop, and not baby talk, but happy adult talk. My God, does Bob have a way with kids. She and Bob were actually having a conversation. She had an amazing vocabulary for a two-year old. From what I've read, her natural parents were a couple of really bright people.

"Who you?" Tilly asked.

"I'm Daddy," Bob said with the biggest smile I'd ever seen on his face. He pointed toward me in the kitchen. "That's Mommy."

"Hi, Daddy, hi Mommy."

I melted.

Bob had also ordered some clothing for her, and I was amazed at how well they fit. I guess being a detective for so long, Bob has acquired a talent for sizing up measurements.

Neither of us wanted to stop hugging her, but we realized that it was best we let her walk on her own as much as possible. I set the table and said, "Come on over Tilly,"

She hobbled over and tried to crawl onto a chair. Bob pointed toward a highchair and said, "Let Daddy put you in there."

"Thank you, Daddy."

I set out some cold cuts and salad for Bob and me and put a bowl of oatmeal in front of Tilly. Although I have no idea how to cook, it looks like I'm going to need to learn. I sure have a reason to now.

"How do you like Mommy's oatmeal, honey?" Bob said. *Mommy*. I love the sound of that word.

"Good!" she said. I had been holding my breath. I guess even *I* can't screw up oatmeal.

"Where's Mama and Papa?" Tilly asked.

Bob put his arm around her, kissed her cheek, and said, "They're in heaven looking down at you. They sent Mommy and me to take care of you."

I always think of Bob as a tough cop. Tilly brings out the softness in him. Watching Bob with Tilly reminds me how much I love this man.

Later that afternoon, a babysitter named Jane Romelli came to the door. She had been highly recommended by a few cops at One PP.

Jane is a novelist and is working on her second book. She lives right nearby. This gives her flexibility to take care of Tilly on a moment's notice if Bob and I need to run to a crime scene. We gave her one of the four guest bedroom suites as her own for whenever she would stay over. I couldn't have been happier at Tilly's reaction to Jane and at Jane's reaction to Tilly. When we interviewed her, we learned that Jane was an orphan, having lost her parents to a car accident when she was six years old. She spent many years in different foster homes. I think that gives her a special appreciation for our Tilly.

Bob and I stood there hugging each other as we watched Jane and Tilly play with her new toys.

We've had some wonderfully happy times in our marriage. Now we can share those times with our extended family, our Tilly.

I plan to return to work after another week. I wonder what mayhem awaits us. It can wait. I just want to get to know our gorgeous little daughter.

CHAPTER 7

George Flynn enjoyed his subway ride from Manhattan on the IRT Number 7 train to Flushing, Queens. He was a senior research clerk for the New York City Parks Department located in the old Arsenal Building at the entrance to the Central Park Zoo. His job didn't offer his brain much of a challenge, so he used his train ride to and from home to keep his mind sharp by memorizing the stops on the local and the ever-changing signs of the nearby companies.

Today was August 15, and he recalled his favorite ride on the Number 7 train 54 years ago in 1965 when he was 18 years old. He had just begun his job as an intern at the Parks Department. The doors opened at the Willets Point-Shea Stadium stop (now called Mets-Willets Point). To this day he remembered that the car was filled with the voice of John Lennon singing "Can't Buy Me Love" at the historic Beatles Concert at Shea Stadium. The train erupted in voices singing along with the Beatles. George Flynn's was one of those voices. The Number 7 train was more than just a means of transportation, at least it was for George Flynn. The Number 7 was *his* train, his memories, his history. Yes, I can't buy me love, but I can buy me a ticket on the Number 7.

Flynn loves New York City, especially the somewhat suburban county of Queens, where he grew up and lives to this day in the Bayside section. He especially loves the public transportation around the city.

Wherever you are, you're not far from a subway train or a bus. With his modest-paying job, Flynn was content to let others worry about paying parking fees, insurance, gas, and monthly car payments. And public transportation was well-known to be safe.

The next and last stop was Roosevelt Avenue, which emptied onto Main Street, Flushing and its buses to everywhere.

Hey, where the hell does this guy think he's going? Flynn thought with a sudden jolt of fear. The entrance to the Roosevelt Avenue station begins with a long curved and sloping track, which, as he recalled too well, was always negotiated slowly. But this train was hurtling toward Roosevelt Avenue like a rocket on tracks.

George Flynn came out of his coma at Flushing Hospital two weeks later, having suffered a life-threatening concussion. He asked a nurse to hand him a mirror as she poured him a glass of water.

"Drink this first, and then hold your breath," she said.

He looked into the mirror and thought he'd lose consciousness again. The face he looked at he didn't recognize. His eyes were swollen slits, his nose badly broken. He didn't want to count the colors he saw in the mirror. He looked down and saw that his left arm was in a cast.

The nurse took the mirror, placed it in the drawer of the end table, and fluffed up his pillow.

"How do you feel, Mr. Flynn? We were worried about you. For

a couple of weeks there we thought we might lose you. I'm glad to hear you speaking."

"What happened?"

"Let's see how your memory is doing. Tell me the last thing you can remember."

"John Lennon singing 'Can't Find Me Love.' No wait, that was a long time ago. The last thing I recall was sitting on the Number 7 train. We were coming to the last stop, Roosevelt Avenue. I think the train was speeding. Yes, definitely, the train was going really fast."

"God has a way of taking care of us with short-term amnesia to protect us from horrible memories. Just be happy that you can't remember exactly what happened to you two weeks ago. A lot of people, 250 to be exact, will never have a chance to recall that train ride because they're dead. I just called your wife and she's coming in to see you. She was here this morning, and she's been frantic with your lack of communication."

"My God, subway train accidents are few and far between," Flynn said.

"Correction, they *used to be* few and far between. Your train wreck was the first of four in just two weeks. The MTA is going nuts trying to figure out what's going on. All four crashes involved a sudden acceleration and then a loss of brakes. The train you were on slammed into a parked train at 50 MPH. You had a close scrape with death, Mr. Flynn. I'll let you catch a few winks. Your wife and grandson will be here in a few minutes."

George Flynn felt lucky to be alive.

CHAPTER 8

Bobbie

B ob and I decided to skip our usual breakfast at the diner. We wanted Tilly to get accustomed to eating at home. Maybe when she gets a little older, we'll take her to the diner, but for the near future at least, it's breakfast at home. Bob and I felt like we were in heaven with our beautiful new daughter.

Today will be my first day back at work after convalescing from my head wound. My headaches have virtually disappeared, thank God, and I'm no longer having weird dreams. Jane Romelli, our babysitter, arrived promptly at 7:30 and we sat down to breakfast. Jane insisted on cooking, which was more than fine with me, because I'm clueless when it comes to cooking. Bob often tells me that I make excellent boiled water.

It was a beautiful May morning with a temperature of 78. We decided to have breakfast on our rooftop dining area next to the garden. Tilly sat on Jane's lap, stroking her hair. The view of lower Manhattan is interesting, if not exactly beautiful, but having the sky overhead is a great way to enjoy a meal. We even installed an outdoor kitchen so we wouldn't need to truck food up the one flight to the rooftop. Bob and I both enjoy gardening, strange as that may sound about a couple of city people. Our rooftop living area sports lovely shrubs and flowers around the perimeter next to an outdoor running track.

This will be our first day away from Tilly, but we feel confident that Jane is the lady for the job. We saw her genuine affection for Tilly, and Tilly's for her. The way she looks at Tilly and plays with her makes us happy that we hired her.

But now it's back to One PP and the mayhem of law enforcement.

CHAPTER 9

Bobbie

After breakfast with Tilly and Jane, Bob and I walked to One Police Plaza, aka One PP. Before we married, Bob bought the building of eight two-bedroom apartments. He had inherited $10 million from a rich uncle and made a wise investment. Then we wrote a book together entitled *Detectiving*. Weird name, but not weird financially. The editor at Random House was impressed by our credentials and made us a book-deal offer. We got a $15 million advance, and the book is now bringing in about $100,000 a month in royalties. My talented partner had also written a best-selling novel before we met: *An Army of Blue – Stories of New York Cops*. It racks up about $25,000 a month in royalties. With our new-found wealth, we bought a beautiful waterfront home in East Hampton, and also renovated our apartment after the next-door tenant moved out. We knocked down the wall, and now have a huge 3,000 square foot apartment with four bedroom suites and our rooftop living area— three blocks from One PP.

So, Bob and I are kind of loaded. But the last thing from our minds is retiring. We're both Detectives First Grade with the NYPD and we love our work. We love being cops. We love to solve puzzles. We also love each other, as well as our new daughter, Tilly. I can't wait to show her our house in East Hampton.

When we walked into our office, I noticed a memo on our desk. We have two desks that face each other. This is an excellent way for two detectives to communicate. It also gives me a wonderful view of Bob's gorgeous hazel eyes, which always calms me. The note from Ralph was scribbled.

Commissioner Ralph likes to use old fashioned handwriting when he wants to convey emotion. When he needs to ring a bell, email just doesn't do it for him. The note told us to report to his office immediately. Bob and I both thought we knew what he wanted to talk about—the horrific crash of the Number 7 train the evening before.

Ralph stood and walked up to us when we entered his office. He gave us each a bear hug. Ralph doesn't hide his emotions. He isn't just our boss; he's our friend, our good friend. Ralph visited me every day in the hospital, but I was unconscious most of the time. On Saturday he and his wife Marlene came to our apartment to meet Tilly, armed with a large bag of toys. They were both happy for us and our new little girl.

"You look tired, Ralph," I said. He insists that we call him Ralph, not commissioner.

"I've been up since four. I guess you guys have figured out what I want you to work on."

We both said, "The train crash?"

"What else?" Ralph said.

"But do you suspect a crime?" I said. "Train accidents usually involve some faulty equipment or maybe human error. Does anybody suspect that maybe the operator was drunk? But even if he was under the influence, wouldn't the MTA police be able to handle this? I'm surprised that they contacted the NYPD so soon."

Ralph reached out and handed us two 8 ½ by 11 pieces of paper which both had the same words, all in bold caps:

THE CITY OF NEW YORK WILL SOON STOP MOVING

I noticed specks of dried blood on both sheets of paper.

"These messages were found strewn all around the train in question," Ralph said. "You've heard the story by now, I'm sure. Dozens of witnesses said the train speeded up as it approached the Roosevelt Avenue station, and there was no apparent application of brakes. The MTA engineers work fast, I'm impressed to see. The engineers immediately focused on that evidence and found that the throttle and brakes were in working order. That fact, combined with those flyers, make us believe that there's criminality involved. Somebody made this shit happen. It wasn't an accident."

"And the part of that message that said '…will soon stop moving,' tells us that this won't be the last incident," Bob said. "It almost seems like terrorism."

"Definitely looks like terrorism," Ralph said. "That fucking train crashed into a parked train at 50 mph. Over 250 people have been killed. And you're right, Bob. The words '…will soon stop moving,' tells us that more shit is on its way toward the fan. I never tell you two how to work, but I suggest that you visit the hospitals and interview the survivors. There isn't a lot a couple of detectives can do staring at a crumpled subway train. The MTA investigators will send us technical information as they uncover it. Have at it, guys. You are now the official lead detectives on this case for the NYPD. If there ever was a case for the BBs, this is it."

Ralph coined the phrase *BBs* to refer to Bob and me two years ago. I kind of love it. Bob and Bobbie—the BBs. In an article in *The New York Times*, our nickname made its public debut. The article was entitled, "The BBs – New York City's Dynamic Detective Duo." That article helped land us the big book contract.

This case looks like a bitch of a puzzle. That's okay; the BBs are good at puzzles. As Bob loves to say, "Now it's *our* bitch."

CHAPTER 10

Bob

B obbie and I agreed with Ralph that our time will be best spent interviewing passengers from the ill-fated Number 7 train. Even after a scene of chaos, sometimes an observant witness can put you on the right path. We will start at Flushing Hospital, where most of the injured passengers were taken. When we walked into the emergency room, we felt as if we were hit by a baseball bat. I had spent six hellish months in Fallujah Province in Iraq when I was a Marine captain. I've seen my share of crowded hospitals. In Iraq we were subject to the constant threat of IEDs (improvised explosive devices). Every day, soldiers and Marines would lose their lives and limbs to the buried explosives. We also were under the regular threat of rifle and mortar attacks.

But we never faced death and destruction by the trainload. Flushing Hospital made the field hospitals in Iraq look like convalescent centers. The walls were lined with gurneys and severely injured people. In our line of work, Bobbie and I see some pretty gruesome stuff. But I've never seen anything as intense as the hallways of

Flushing Hospital that morning. The sounds of groans were punctuated by an occasional scream. Doctors and nurses hustled from person to person, trying to save as many lives as possible. I noticed a doctor pull a sheet over a patient's head, the poor man obviously having just died. We huddled closely with the head nurse and listened to her advice on which patients were in good enough shape to be interviewed. Any time Bobbie and I interview people in a hospital, we always defer to the medical staff. As we spoke to her, the chief surgeon walked over to us.

"Nancy," the chief surgeon said, "our job is to save lives, but I just want to let you know that these two detectives are vital to prevent another goddam scene like this. Tell all the nurses to give Detectives Lawton and Nelson their full cooperation."

Bobbie and I were happy that the doctor in charge gets it. He knows that law enforcement is critical unless he wants to see his hospital regularly packed wall to wall with wounded and dying people.

Over the years, Bobbie and I have developed a sixth sense of who would be likely to openly communicate. By mid-day we had questioned a dozen passengers. Most had little to say, other than describe the chaos as their bodies were flung through the air. Imagine sitting or standing on a train that suddenly goes from 50 mph to zero in a split second. The train stops, but your body doesn't.

We were looking for one key piece of evidence—whether anybody saw someone tossing the flyers—*The City of New York Will Soon Stop Moving.* Or better yet, maybe someone could describe that person. At 2 p.m. we hit pay dirt, or at least we hoped it was. As a couple of detectives who have been around the block a few times, Bobbie and I brace ourselves for disappointment when we think we've found a major clue, because often what seems like a major clue turns out to be nothing. We were interviewing a 22-year-old woman, Karen Solomon. Her face was badly bruised, and her right arm was in a cast, but she was in pretty decent shape, considering what she had gone through. She had a bright, friendly personality, and seemed to want to talk to us. I think she was just happy to be alive. When we inquired about the flyers, she reached over to the end table, winced in pain, and grabbed her cellphone.

"This guy totally freaked me out," Karen said. "I had no idea what he was doing, until I heard about those flyers. I didn't get hold of one on the train because I was unconscious at the time. Here, take a look."

The video on her phone showed a man about three feet from her with his back against the forward compartment wall as if he was bracing himself for something. He seemed to be wearing heavy padding under his clothes. He also appeared to be wearing makeup. There was something about his nose that didn't look like it was his. We watched as the guy reached into a briefcase, with a latex glove on one hand, and came out with a bunch of sheets of paper. He looked at his watch, and then flung the flyers out into the car. People must have been confused, because until that time nothing had happened—yet. The video suddenly stopped as Karen and her phone were hurtled forward.

Karen then emailed the video to Bobbie and me at my request. We would then bring the video to the police lab where still photos would be made, and the image would be put through facial recognition software. We would then take the video and the still photos and interview the passengers we had already spoken to, as well as more at Queens General Hospital, another location where dozens of wounded passengers were taken. I had one nagging thought. His face *did* appear to be heavily made up. But at least we had a video and photos. We thanked Karen and continued room to room, constantly touching base with the head nurse as to who was in shape to be interviewed. On orders from the chief surgeon, she gave us her full cooperation. She also seemed to understand that Bobbie and I know what we're doing.

At 4:30 we came upon a male passenger who recognized the man from the video. He was heavily sedated, but communicative enough to talk. I noticed that he was missing his left leg from the hip down.

"Did the man say anything?" Bobbie asked.

"Yes, he shouted 'Alahu Akbar.' "

CHAPTER 11

Bobbie

By 5:30 p.m., Bob and I had interviewed every passenger at Flushing Hospital who was able to talk. We returned to our apartment at 6:15 and showered. Nothing like hanging around all day in a hospital that makes you want to shower. Jane said good night as I gathered little Tilly in my arms. It's only been eight hours, but I missed her already. We ate a light dinner in our apartment, neither of us feeling very hungry. I called in for a delivery from a nearby gourmet deli. I should really learn how to cook. Screw it. God gave us telephones for a reason. The deli even has a children's menu.

Bob clicked on the TV so we could catch the latest news.

"Wolf Blitzer for *CNN,* ladies and gentlemen. Just as our city is still reeling from that horrific train crash yesterday, we are faced with another story of horrible death and injuries. The Number 4 train of the IRT Dyer Avenue Line crashed into a stopped train at the Woodlawn Avenue station in the Bronx. We've been telling you for hours that yesterday's crash of the Number 7 train outside of Flushing was the worst subway crash in New York City history. Well, that record has been broken this evening. Over 325 people have been killed and the injured number over 400, many critical. The details are eerily familiar. Just as with the Number 7 train, eyewitnesses have come forward saying that the train suddenly accelerated to a high rate of speed, and nobody felt any brakes being applied. MTA records show that the train was moving at 50 miles per hour. Also, there is the subject of the strange flyers that were found strewn about. Just as with the Number 7 train crash, the flyers read: *THE CITY OF NEW YORK WILL SOON STOP MOVING.* If anyone watching has any idea about those flyers, or if you have any information about the crashes at all, please report it immediately to the police at the 800 number you see at the bottom of the screen. Stay tuned to *CNN* for updates on these terrible tragedies."

The phone rang and I picked up. It was Joyce Reynolds, our junior detective assistant at the NYPD. Bob and I consider ourselves blessed to have such a bright assistant. She's not only smart but has limitless patience for wading through evidence. Diligent could be her middle name.

"They found the guy throwing the flyers, Bobbie," Joyce said. "He's dead. And you and Bob were right; he was heavily made up. The facial recognition technicians are at the morgue right now. When the medical examiner removes the makeup, maybe we can get a handle on who the guy was. I guess you heard about the other train crash. Hey, turn on your TV to *Fox News.*"

"Shepard Smith for *Fox News*, ladies and gentlemen. Just as we've been trying to wrap our heads around those two horrible train wrecks in the past 24 hours, I have yet another shocking story about sickening mayhem on public transportation. The Q44 bus was crossing the Bronx-Whitestone Bridge on its way to the Bronx when it suddenly accelerated, went out of control, and struck the side of the bridge with such force that it sent the bus over the rail into the East River below. The Coast Guard is on the scene looking for any possible survivors on the bus. The outlook is grim because the bus immediately sank. The Bronx-Whitestone Bridge, built in 1939, has undergone extensive damage and will be closed for as long as six weeks. Motorists are advised to use the nearby Throgs Neck Bridge until further notice. In other news…"

"Bob, we're watching New York City come apart at the seams," I said. "All this shit happened in the past 24 hours. I don't doubt that soon people will stop using public transportation because they're afraid of getting killed."

"Yeah, Bobbie, that flyer found at the scenes says it all: *Soon the City of New York Will Stop Moving.* The obvious objective is to cripple the city, if it isn't crippled already. We've got to stop this scumbag."

"Hey, Bob, we should watch our language. We don't want Tilly to grow up sounding like a cop."

Tilly was sitting on Bob's lap, stroking his lips as he talked. I've been a dedicated cop for many years but looking at our little Tilly suddenly gave me even more reason to stop the mayhem in the world.

"Bob, I think we're looking at a group of people, a group of terrorists. They found those flyers on every car on the trains. One guy couldn't pull that off."

"You're right, hon, we're looking at a group."

"What worries me Bob, is that you and I are great at solving cases. But usually it's *after* the fact. This shit is different. Whoops, I mean this stuff. We don't want to solve these cases after thousands of people are killed. If we don't head this off, we'll be looking at a war zone. I'm feeling totally stressed out."

Bob smiled and wrapped his arms around me. He has a way of de-stressing me. We kissed, a long, slow, deep kiss. No matter how shitty I feel, Bob's arms around me snaps me out of it. I had just tucked Tilly into bed, and she fell fast asleep. As Bob hugged me I could feel his growing erection pressing against me, telling me that Bob is thinking about making love.

"Hey, Bob, we should shower and go to bed."

"But I'm not tired."

"Neither am I," I said as I kicked off my shoes and undid his belt. "I'm not tired at all."

Bob and I know how to handle stress.

CHAPTER 12

Bob

Two weeks later, Bobbie and I met with Molly Tiverton, New York City Department of Transportation Commissioner in Mayor Paxton's office. NYPD Commissioner Norquist was with us. We had been to the mayor's office many times before, and we were always impressed that it was so neat. Mayor Paxton has a reputation for orderliness, not to mention decisiveness. A scale model of a NYC subway car was on his desk. The mayor is well-known for bringing drama to a meeting. It was pouring rain as we could see through the window. It somehow seemed fitting for the gloominess of the meeting.

In the past 10 days there was another train attack, this one in Brooklyn, bringing the total to three. All three wrecks bore the same imprints: a sudden acceleration and no application of brakes. There were also five more crashes involving buses.

Mayor Arnold Paxton is a tall, handsome black man at 6'3". He didn't seem his normal energetic self. He looked like he hadn't slept in days, and Bobbie mentioned it to him. We've gotten to know the mayor and his wife quite well. We handled the case last year when they were kidnapped. That case was scary as hell. A few months ago, they spent a weekend at our house in East Hampton.

"I'm going to ask Commissioner Molly here to bring us up to date on the status of our city's transportation," the mayor said.

"This shit is officially out of control," Molly Tiverton said. She's well known for her blunt and sometimes off-color manner of speaking. Molly is 55 years old and speaks with an intensity that adds to her attractive face. "In the past two weeks, ridership on New York City buses and subway trains is down 90 percent. The result, among other things, is total gridlock in the city's streets. The death toll in these attacks is now over 1,200, a horrible statistic. Just as with airports after 9/11, every person now goes through a metal detector before boarding a bus or train. That further compounds the gridlock problem, to say the least. People have grown accustomed to hopping on a bus or train and finding a seat. Those days are over. Now each passenger is stopped and frisked before boarding. Just going to work is proving to be an ordeal. Suddenly we're living in a different city."

"Commissioner Ralph was smart to assign the two best detectives in the NYPD to these cases," the mayor said. "Anything you folks can tell us, Bob and Bobbie? By the way, congratulations on your new little bundle of joy. Ralph showed me her picture."

"Thank you, sir. Yes, our little Tilly *is* a bundle of joy. The video that we were given of the man throwing flyers has turned up a result, but not the outcome we were hoping for," I said. "As you know, the man was killed when another passenger was flung against him. The medical examiner removed his makeup, and using facial recognition software, we determined the man's name is Mustaffa Reezin, and that he hailed from Yemen. He was on the watch list of both the CIA and the FBI. That tells us he was a potential terrorist."

"*Potential* terrorist?" The mayor said. "Hey, Bob, don't be politically correct. The scumbag was a terrorist and his actions proved it."

"I think Commissioner Molly's idea of installing surveillance cameras on all buses and trains is an excellent one," Bobbie said.

"Well, maybe," Molly said, "but the process has just begun, and the expense is enormous."

"Let's not worry about the expense," Mayor Paxton said. "It's something we need to do no matter what the cost. I've got to get this city moving again."

"Mr. Mayor, I suggest you turn on the TV and click to *CBS*," his assistant said.

"Norah O'Donnell for *CBS News*, ladies and gentlemen. Our horrible reports of attacks on public transportation continue unabated. We have just received word that a Long Island Railroad commuter train has derailed after crashing into a smaller train parked on a siding at the Jamaica station of the LIRR. With this attack, it appears that the entire Metropolitan Transportation Authority is under siege. Before this it was only subway trains and buses. I will be interrupting our normal programming to bring you updates on this terrifying story. The number of train wrecks is now up to four. In other news…"

"Did I mention that I don't care about the cost?" the mayor said.

"With your approval, sir, I recommend that we hire personnel from across the country to install surveillance cameras," Molly Tiverton said. "I want to move as quickly as possible."

"What do you folks from the NYPD think about that?" Paxton said.

I didn't want to pour cold water on this idea with my Marine Corps combat background, but I felt I needed to be blunt with everyone.

"Yes, surveillance cameras are a great idea," I said, "but that doesn't stop a guy hiding in the bushes from firing a rocket-propelled grenade." I once went through that very experience.

The silence in the room after my comment was deafening. Everyone stared at me, including Bobbie. Looks like I threw a damper on our gathering. Mayor Paxton adjourned the meeting.

CHAPTER 13

Bob

A t 6:15, Bobbie and I arrived back home from our office. Jane had prepared our dinner, including a special menu for Tilly. Jane loves to cook and is great at it. Maybe she can give Bobbie and me some lessons. Our meeting with the mayor was just that, a meeting. Molly Tiverton did come up with the idea to enlist help from around the country to rig all public transportation vehicles with surveillance cameras. She's a sharp commissioner, and her idea was a good one, but then I pointed out that a guy hidden in the bushes with an RPG launcher would render all the surveillance cameras worthless.

"Hey, Bob, why don't you mix us a couple of martinis while we're pretending to relax."

Yeah, *pretending to relax*. If there's one thing Bobbie and I have in common, it's that we like to solve cases, which means bringing to a close whatever shit we're working on. We take our work personally, and we want to put a stop to the killings. But she's right.

We need to take a deep breath and slow down. The entire city, not to mention the country, is on red alert. The bodies are mounting up, and unless we can stop this, it will continue. The CIA and FBI are on the case as well, which is no surprise. Bobbie and I are used to dealing with the feds, and we respect them. Hell, we've been deputized as provisional agents in both agencies many times, and we know that they trust us. Since that guy tossing out the flyers died, we've hit a dry hole. Whoever is involved in this mass murder is cautious—*extremely cautious*. But Bobbie and I are getting impatient.

We're up to four train wrecks in two weeks. Over 1,400 people have been killed, and a lot more seriously wounded. Add to that the bus crashes with another 525 dead. The most recent train crash was a mirror image of the previous two. The train suddenly accelerated, and the brakes didn't work, or weren't applied. The Number 5 train, the Lexington Avenue Express, crashed into a parked freight train at the Brooklyn College station in Midwood. That was crash number three and was followed the next day by the Long Island Railroad train wreck at Jamaica station, bringing the number up to four. Bobbie and I decided to go to the scene and try to find an investigative engineer who could talk to us. We have a pattern to investigate—sudden acceleration and no brakes.

We didn't know it at the time, but what we would hear would shock the hell out of us.

CHAPTER 14

Maria Carlucci had just taken a job as an associate professor of English at Brooklyn College, after the current professor suddenly decided to retire. She expected to get her PhD at Columbia the following year, and she couldn't be happier to land a college teaching position. She had dreamed of teaching college for all her young adult life. Her parents threw a big party for her when they heard the news. Her boyfriend bought her an expensive leather briefcase. Maria felt like she was on top of the world. A college teaching job!

Maria boarded the Number 5 Lexington Avenue Express at Eastchester in the Bronx. Few people were on the train that morning, many frightened by the recent subway train crashes. She looked at the subway map on the overhead in front of her and saw that they were approaching the Brooklyn College stop. She was surprised that the train suddenly accelerated. Oh my God, she thought, as she recalled the news reports of the recent crashes. She always thought of herself as a positive-minded person and didn't hesitate to board the train that morning despite the recent reports. Maria was seated in the middle of the car. Holy shit this train is going fast, she thought. It's picking up speed.

"Brace yourselves," screamed the operator, "prepare for impact!"

Maria was propelled through the air and her head slammed into the forward wall of the car at 50 mph. In the final moment of her life, she felt sad that she'd never teach a college class.

CHAPTER 15

Bobbie

B ob and I called for a car to take us to the scene of the Number 5 train crash near Brooklyn College. Although detectives normally do their own driving, our friend and boss, Ralph, is a big fan of ours and we now rate a driver. He wants our brains to concentrate on solving cases, not on traffic. Jane showed up at 8 a.m. and we left after hugging Tilly. We couldn't be happier with Jane as our babysitter. She obviously loves Tilly and Tilly reciprocates. Whenever Jane walks through the door, Tilly claps her hands and yells, "Janey." The fact that she's a fabulous cook was an unanticipated bonus.

The scene, as we expected, was one of horrible mayhem. The entire train of seven cars derailed, of course, by the force of the collision. As we reached the bottom of the steps, we noticed that the last car of the train had jumped the platform and was lying on its side, looking like a wounded animal. Body bags, more than I wanted to count, lined the nearby wall. The screams of the wounded and dying is difficult to describe. If pain has a sound, we heard it. Bob and I wore our NYPD shields, but we kept our distance and deferred to the medical personnel.

Transportation Commissioner Molly had given us the cellphone number of Henry Browner, the chief investigator for the MTA. Bob and I had met him once before and we like him. He's friendly and cooperative and knows the urgency of the NYPD's involvement. He's not full of himself as many engineering investigators are. He also has a good sense of humor, always a welcome characteristic when you work a crime scene. I phoned him and he told us where he was located at the site.

"Hey, Bob and Bobbie, welcome to my latest cluster fuck," Henry (Hank) said. "I'm happy that the police commissioner has assigned the BBs to these wrecks, because we sure as hell need the best minds in the NYPD on the case. You guys can tap into my brain while I tap into yours."

"Hank, Bob and I may have a dumb question, but we're not engineers so we'll ask it anyway," I said. "In the four wrecks so far, they all show the same fact pattern—a sudden acceleration and no application of brakes. Unfortunately, the operators on these crashes are all dead, but do you think they may be implicated?"

"No, it's not a dumb question, Bobbie, and it's the immediate conclusion that seems apparent. Often a train wreck is the result of human error, sometimes compounded by intoxication. But we've found some technical evidence that has us flipping out. On all four trains we found high intensity radio beacon transmitters located in the first car. And I do mean *high* intensity. These devices are used by the Army to jam electronics in enemy tanks. I had a hunch, so I called a friend who is the senior engineering officer for the 82nd Airborne Division. We were classmates at MIT. I flew down to meet him at Fort Bragg with one of the devices. He confirmed what I suspected. One of these transmitters can be used to overcome a train's throttle mechanism as well as its brakes. But it first takes some high-powered engineering to make it happen. Yes, the people who are pulling off this shit are technically sophisticated, amazingly sophisticated."

"Hank," Bob said, "can these radio transmitters work on buses as well, accelerating the vehicle and disarming the brakes, just like on the trains?"

"Yes, Bob, they can work on buses as well. We found one of these transmitters on each of the five bus crash sites. We've got our work cut out for us."

"Hank, here's a question," I said. "You said that these devices are used by the Army to disable enemy tanks. Do you know who we can ask if there have been any thefts of the transmitters?"

"I'll put you in touch with my friend Lt. Colonel Frank Billings at Fort Bragg, the guy who told me about the anti-tank transmitters. If he doesn't know about any thefts, I'm sure he can point you in the right direction. Frank's a good guy and I'm sure he'll help you in any way he can."

I called Colonel Billings after Hank had alerted him. Billings told me to contact Brigadier General Wayne Tucker at the Pentagon, the man responsible for all Army electronic warfare. I immediately called FBI Director Sarah Watson and asked her to place a call for us. It always helps to have some high-powered introductions.

We called our babysitter Jane and told her that we would need to fly to Washington that afternoon, not wanting to waste any time. Jane said it's no problem. Jane, God bless her, should have "flexibility" as her middle name. And she loves the guest room where she stays. Most importantly, she loves our Tilly. As Tilly sleeps, Jane works on her next novel.

Commissioner Ralph requested FBI Director Sarah Watson to assign an FBI Gulfstream jet to Bob and me for the remainder of the investigation. He didn't want us waiting on flight schedules. The Gulfstream G650 is a beautiful twin engine jet that can accommodate up to 19 people, but only Bob and I would make up the passenger list. I was reminded of the TV show, *Criminal Minds*, where a group of FBI agents jet around the country in a private jet. Bob and I agreed that we felt like hot shit. Wow, our own Gulfstream.

We touched down at Reagan International Airport and our pilot taxied the Gulfstream to a restricted area. We then took the five-minute ride to the Pentagon in a vehicle assigned to us. Both Bob and I had been to the Pentagon before, but only as tourists.

We were escorted to General Tucker's office by an armed guard. Our NYPD shields didn't impress the security devices at the Pentagon, and we went through a constant array of buzzing, beeping, and clanging devices.

General Wayne Tucker heads up the US Army Electronics Warfare Division. Tucker was somewhat short at 5'6", slim with a ramrod stance. He looked about in his mid-50s. His office was surprisingly large. I guess if you're a brigadier general, you rate some extra space.

He stood to greet us and shook our hands

"It's a pleasure to meet you folks," he said. "I've read quite a bit about you. I also read that Bob here is a highly decorated former Marine Captain. I'm honored. FBI Director Watson told me that you would be in touch. So, what can I do for you?"

"Bob and I are in charge of the investigation of the public transportation attacks in New York. An investigative engineer for the Metropolitan Transportation Authority told us that this device has been used to disable the throttle and braking mechanisms on trains."

I reached into my bag and withdrew the transmitter. It is barely the size of a lightweight backpack. My research told me that the unit comes with two primary capabilities: VROD (Versatile Radio Observation & Direction) to "detect and understand" enemy electromagnetic signals, and the so-called VMAX to "search and attack" with "electronic attack effects" that the Army described as "more effective than the existing jammers used by anti-missile systems in aircraft."

"Oh my God," General Tucker said, "that device is one of the most sophisticated weapons we've ever developed. It can disable an enemy tank without firing a shot. And you're telling me that it's being used against civilian targets, specifically trains and buses?"

"Yes, sir," Bob said. "These devices were found at the scene of all four train crashes, as we'll as the scenes of five bus crashes. And we believe they were stolen from the US Army."

"Well, that's highly classified but under the circumstances I'll be straight with you, especially because you were referred to me by the Director of the FBI. In the past two months, no fewer than 40 of the devices have been stolen. We're seeing the most intense investigation the Army has ever launched. In the wrong hands those devices can be lethal on a mass scale. I'm afraid that the New York transit system is in for some dark days."

"Have you arrested any suspects, General?" I said.

"Yes, only one. His name is Ali Munir, until recently a sergeant in the US Army. He's being held at Fort Leavenworth. He hasn't responded to any questions, but from what I've heard about your interrogation skills, maybe he'll open up to you. I'll personally call the commandant of the prison and let him know you're coming."

We thanked General Tucker profusely. My God, this could be the best lead we've had. Bob and I didn't want to spare a minute of time, but it was getting late and we stayed over in Washington. I told our Gulfstream pilot that we'd fly to Fort Leavenworth, Kansas the next morning. I invited him to have dinner with Bob and me. Thank God our babysitter, Jane, loves our apartment. She keeps a three-change set of clothes in her guestroom. A good thing because she'll be staying over often for the balance of this investigation. I called Jane and asked to speak to Tilly, who seemed happy to hear from me. "Hi Mommy," she said, causing my heart to miss a beat.

CHAPTER 16

Bob

We landed at Kansas City International Airport the next morning at 11 a.m., 17 miles from Fort Leavenworth. We told our driver to take us to the charmingly-named United States Disciplinary Barracks, one of the three prisons at Fort Leavenworth, this one designated maximum security. We were led inside by a corporal wearing sidearm with an M16 slung over his shoulder. A man wearing the bars of a colonel greeted us in the lobby. He introduced himself as Colonel Max Durmand, the commandant of the prison. General Tucker had personally called him to let him know we were on our way, as he had promised. Nothing like friends in high places to move the action forward.

Colonel Max led us to the interrogation room where we would meet Ali Munir, our w. I've been in a lot of prisons over the years, but this one was different. Instead of prisoners shouting obscenities at you, the halls were quiet, nothing like the hellhole on Rikers Island in New York. I recalled the time when Bobbie and I interrogated a couple of suspects at Rikers.

Whenever I think of the place, I feel the need for a shower. The military, on the other hand, likes things neat, and strict enforcement of the rules is the natural order of things.

The prisoner was already in the room, his hands and feet shackled to the table in front of him. Bobbie and I agreed that I would begin the interrogation in case Mr. Munir had an issue with being questioned by a woman. Tough shit. I would begin, but Bobbie would immediately join in the questioning. Nobody interrogates people like Bobbie.

Ali Munir was a slightly built man with a dark complexion. His hair was still short in Army fashion. From what we'd read about him, he was 29 years old, and was born and raised in Saudi Arabia. He spoke English with only a slight Arab accent.

"Mr. Munir, my name is Detective Bob Lawton and this is my partner, Detective Bobbie Nelson. As you know you have been accused of the theft of Army transmitting devices. We found nine such devices at crime scenes in New York City, four on trains and five on buses. Do you wish to comment on that?"

"I don't know what you are talking about," Munir said, pretty much as we expected.

"I'm sure you understand that Colonel Durmand has discussed the subject of leniency with your court-appointed attorney. Unless you wish to remain in prison for the rest of your life, I suggest that you be open with us. Detective Nelson and I are trying to prevent the deaths of innocent people. So, let me rephrase my question. Do you have any idea how those transmitting devices could have found their way to New York City subway trains and buses?"

"I gave them to my brothers. They told me the devices would be used to disable subway trains and buses."

I looked at Bobbie, indicating that she should join in the questioning.

"Mr. Munir, are you aware that the devices didn't just disable the trains and buses, but rather turned them into weapons of massive death and destruction." Bobbie said. "The transmitters first speeded up the train or bus and then disabled the brakes, causing it to crash at a high rate of speed, resulting in an enormous loss of life."

Munir stared at us as if he'd just received an electric shock. Bobbie and I have become experts at reading people's faces, and we can tell when somebody is bullshitting us. This guy wasn't acting, wasn't trying to put one over on us. Bobbie obviously shocked the shit out of him when she told him about the train and bus wrecks, and how they were caused by the devices he had stolen.

"But the brothers told me the devices would only disable the trains and buses, not destroy them." He looked as if he were about to cry.

"What are the names of these people you refer to as brothers?" I asked.

"If I give you their names, I will be killed."

"Nonsense, they will have no idea their names came from you. Also, I'm sure you're aware that I have the power to change your custody to solitary confinement." That, of course, was complete bullshit. I have no such authority, but I had no hesitancy to lying to this creep to get him to open up and talk.

"So, answer Detective Lawton's question, Mr. Munir," Bobbie said. "How many 'brothers' are there and what are their names?"

"There are only two, Mustaffa Chudri and Muhammed Beezin."

"And where do they live?"

"They both live in Brooklyn."

"Excuse me, I need to visit the ladies' room," Bobbie said. I knew what she was doing. She was going to call Joyce Randolph, our talented detective assistant, to see if she could track down the names.

"Were you paid by those two brothers to steal the transmitters?" Bobbie asked.

"Yes, they paid me $25,000."

"And how many did you steal? Hey, Mr. Munir, look at me and answer my question." I said. "How many did you steal?"

"Forty, altogether."

Bobbie and I continued to interrogate Ali Munir for another hour. We got little additional useful information. But we did get the information we were after—he confirmed how many devices were stolen and disclosed who did the bribing, which meant who is running the show. We considered the day a wrap and called our pilot to let him know we were on our way. Then we called home to say hello to Tilly.

So, we have the names. But will we be able to find the people attached to those names? I hope our able assistant Joyce Randolph is on her game today.

CHAPTER 17

Bobbie

I have no fucking idea how I could do my job without you two," Ralph said after we walked into his office. "The mayor just called tell me what a great job I'm doing, so I get to bask in *your* glory. I didn't expect anything to come from your interrogation of that guy at Leavenworth, but I've learned never to bet against the BBs. Joyce Randolph tracked down the names. Both of the names he gave you are on the FBI and CIA suspect lists. I had them arrested and got a search warrant for their apartments. Sorry I didn't wait for you guys, but I needed to act fast. Guess what we found in one of the apartments. Thirty-one of those high energy anti-tank transmitters. From what you've discovered, according to your memo, 40 transmitters were stolen from the Army. Four have been used on trains and five on buses, so we know we've got the rest. As usual, the BBs nailed it. You fucking nailed it. I want you to take a few days off and chill at your beach house in East Hampton with your little girl Tilly. You've earned some down time."

I gave Ralph a big hug. Yes, Bob and I can use some down time.

CHAPTER 18

Bob

Whan Ralph told us that they found all of the remaining anti-tank transmitters, Bobbie and I couldn't have been happier—or prouder. Our interrogation of that guy in Leavenworth wrapped up the case. Bobbie and I know our shit.

Now we're headed to our vacation home in East Hampton, along with Jane and our little Tilly. With our huge royalties from the sales of our book, *Detectiving*, plus the royalties from my first novel, compounded by my inheritance from my rich uncle and our combined salaries, we had a few bucks to throw around. And we did just that.

A while back, Lorie Fitzgerald, a real estate broker friend of Ralph's, showed us an East Hampton house that took our breaths away. It's a huge two-story beauty of 8,000 square feet, situated on an acre of property on scenic Georgica Pond, a 290-acre lagoon on the border of East Hampton and Wainscott in Eastern Suffolk County. I recalled that President Bill Clinton used Stephen Spielberg's house on Georgica Pond as his summer White House. The house has a long, elegant, sloping roof. The shingling is classic New England, but the five-year-old house looks almost new. Next to the swimming pool is a tastefully designed pool house that matched the roof lines of the home. The entrance hallway has a vaulted ceiling over which was a large roof skylight. I have never seen a more dramatic entrance.

The gym looked like a commercial exercise club with every type of equipment you can imagine. Four large TV screens adorned the walls. Bobbie and I like to watch TV as we work out, and we have a view from every piece of equipment. About 50 feet from the gym is what can best be described as a playroom. It boasts a ping pong table, three card tables, and a huge pool table. Until we came upon the pool table, neither of us was aware that we both love to pay pool, and we're both good at it. Bobbie, with her devilish imagination, came up with the idea of playing "strip billiards." Don't ask. The wall panels were made of sumptuous cherry wood.

The kitchen is gigantic. A few weeks ago, Bobbie and I hosted a party of 50 people. The space was so large the entire party happened in that room.

Each of the eight bedrooms is *en suite,* with an elegant modern full bath included. There is also a master bedroom suite on the first floor, which will probably come in handy if Bobbie and I grow old in this place. The master suite upstairs always takes our breaths away, with its lovely view of Georgica Pond beyond the second-floor deck. It's almost all glass, with windows and sliding doors leading onto the deck. In the bathroom is a hot tub. Bobbie and I *love* hot tubs. A small kitchenette is the perfect spot to make coffee to sip on the deck and look at the water. In the hallway outside the master suite is a large closet—which houses a sauna.

The furniture is beautiful, but neither Bobbie nor I can take credit for that. The place came fully furnished.

When I asked Lorie for the price, I thought I'd choke. Seven million! But then I fought back my choke when I realized that we could easily afford it. God bless book royalties. Bobbie, always the hard bargainer, asked if there was any flexibility on the price. Lorie said what we expected, that the house was priced to sell, and she expected a bidding war when she formally put it on the market.

Case closed. We made the offer and closed on the house in four weeks. Now our ongoing challenge is to find the time to head east.

This visit was a particularly happy one. We handled that Godforsaken war on the MTA, and we were free to relax for a few days. Relax? What a strange word. The sun had just gone down and Tilly was in bed with Jane sitting next to her with her laptop. Bobbie came up with a typically great idea. We would go skinny dipping in the hot tub in our room. We slowly helped each other out of our clothes and climbed into the hot tub. I perched on a platform in the tub as Bobbie wrapped her arms around my neck and smothered my mouth with a kiss only Bobbie can give. Then she straddled me with her beautiful legs and inserted me into her. As always, we began slowly, patiently bringing each other to an amazing orgasm. I glanced out the picture window next to the tub. Just as the full moon peeked out from behind a cloud, we mutually climaxed. We really need to visit here more often.

On Thursday morning my phone sounded. It was Ralph Norquist, calling to say that he and his wife Marlene would be coming to their house, a half-mile away from ours. We planned on dinner at the Palm East Hampton that evening. Jane would stay at the house with Tilly.

Ralph and Marlene pulled up at 6:30 and we climbed into his car to head to the restaurant. We always enjoy socializing with our boss-friend and Marlene. They're great company and crack jokes constantly. I had secured us a table in the back. When we're with Ralph, conversation always gets around to police business, and I wanted privacy.

"Thanks in no small part to you two, our city is over that fucking transit attack crisis," Ralph said. Marlene gave him a gentle slap on the arm as she always does when Ralph's language gets salty.

"Ralph told me all about your efforts in stopping those MTA attacks," Marlene said. "My God, you two are the most amazing detectives on the planet. I'm glad you're on our side."

"Something tells me you've got some fun planned for us, Ralph," Bobbie said.

"Yeah, fun," Ralph said. "Only the BBs could look at the stuff you guys handle as 'fun.' You're right, Bobbie. I do have something big planned for you, something very big. Hey, you're on vacation so I don't want to spoil your relaxation. When you return to One PP, you'll learn all about it."

On Sunday morning we took Jane and Tilly to mass at the local Episcopal church. Jane encouraged Tilly to sing along with the hymns, pointing to each musical notation with her finger. So, besides coaching Tilly to sing, she was teaching her music. After mass we went to breakfast at a nearby restaurant. Bobbie and I have begun to see Jane as our younger sister, definitely part of our happy family.

When Ralph says something is big, it always is. He never exaggerates, so we knew it would be exactly that—big. Sunday afternoon we headed back to the city. Monday we would find out about our new case, a case that would shock the hell out of us.

CHAPTER 19

Mike and Barbara Quinlan sat on the 50-yard line at Memorial Field in Flushing, Queens, to watch the big game between archrivals Holy Cross High School and St. Francis Prep, a major game on the Catholic High School Football League schedule. Their son, Eric, was the starting quarterback for Holy Cross. Mike couldn't have been prouder of Eric, having once been the quarterback at Holy Cross himself. Eric was a tall kid at 6'1," and hoped to win an athletic scholarship to Notre Dame.

Nine hundred and twenty-five people were in attendance. Marching bands for both teams provided the half-time entertainment. At the beginning of the third quarter, the score was tied at 14-14. Eric Quinlan had thrown both touchdown passes for Holy Cross. The early November sky was cloudless, and the temperature was mild at 64 degrees.

"What is that weird sound?" Barbara said. "It sounds like a bunch of angry bees."

A flight of 50 small drones appeared over the billboard. The buzzing sound got louder by the moment. All eyes in the stadium concentrated on the drones.

Eric had just taken the snap from center, and dropped back to pass, hoping to find Mike Peterson, his tight end and best receiver. As he raised his arm to throw, a small 4" by 4" drone crashed into his facemask and exploded, decapitating him. His headless body was splayed across the backfield, the football still gripped in his hand.

Each of the 50 drones, operated by remote control, found its target. Twenty of the aircraft struck the broadcast booth and exploded on impact. No one in the booth survived. The man who was announcing the game was slumped over the edge, blood streaming from his face onto the spectators below. The remaining drones dived toward the stadium seats, about 20 feet apart. Blood and body parts flew skyward in the multiple explosions. Mike and Barbara Quinlan, who had just seen their son Eric die, were themselves killed.

One of the drones flew through the serving window of the food truck, exploding and killing its three occupants.

Bishop Clarence Monahan was in attendance, along with four aides. A graduate of St. Francis, he never missed the big Holy Cross– St. Francis Prep game. A drone struck him in the face and exploded, killing him instantly, along with his companions.

A small flight of drones attacked the Holy Cross marching band, which played during the game, alternating each quarter with the band from St. Francis. An exploding confusion of musical instruments, blood, and body parts ensued.

The fun sounds of a high school football game were replaced by the screams of the wounded and dying, and the wailing of emergency vehicle sirens.

CHAPTER 20

Bobbie

Bob and I walked to One PP the morning after we returned from East Hampton. We just had breakfast with Jane and Tilly. Jane's a fabulous cook and I was happy to see again how much she loves it. We were all nauseated by the horrible news about the attack on that high school football game the afternoon before. My God, who would attack high school kids?

We headed straight for Commissioner Ralph's office as he had requested. Ralph looked as we felt—sickened.

"Believe it or not, but this is the case I had for you guys, although I didn't expect it to get off the ground so soon. Our IT people picked up a lot of instances of large purchases and thefts of aerial drones. We didn't know what it was about, but now we do. Dear Lord, no fewer than 650 people were killed at that high school stadium yesterday. What sick bastard would attack high school kids? I'm sure you guys have been watching this on TV. Any thoughts?"

"Bob and I have been brainstorming nonstop about this, Ralph. I hate to use the word obvious, but it's obvious that this is terrorism. The weird thing is this: terrorism aims to control people's thinking as well as their actions. But who the hell would want to convince people to avoid high school football games? At this point, we have no idea. We've already turned loose our brilliant assistant, Joyce Randolph, on this. Joyce is combing the internet to see if there is any hateful rhetoric about high school football games."

"Do we have any idea where the drones came from?" Bob asked.

"From what we've discovered by examining some drones that didn't explode, they were manufactured by none other than Robot Depot," Ralph said, "the giant corporation that specializes in labor saving devices, including drones. It's a damn fine company, but the world of terror took notice. A few short years ago terrorists began to tamper with their devices and turn them loose on innocent lives. I knew the former CEO of Robot Depot, a hell of a nice guy named Mike Bateman. He couldn't have been more cooperative with law enforcement as we tried to stop his robots from killing people. The poor guy was murdered by a jihadi, beheaded if you can believe that. The company is now run by his widow, Jenny. A lot of people have speculated that Jenny Bateman personally assassinated some of the terrorist big shots. If she did, good for her. The scumbags had it coming. No prosecutor seems interested in going after Jenny Bateman, especially because she's become a sort of folk hero. She even wrote a book entitled *Robot Depot*. If you need to interview her, I'm sure she'd be happy to talk."

"Bob and I will call her."

CHAPTER 21

Bob

obbie and I just pulled up to the Robot Depot headquarters in Hauppauge in Western Suffolk County, Long Island. We have an appointment to meet with Jenny Bateman, the CEO. The Robot Depot "campus" is a 30-acre plot surrounded by beautiful trees and shrubbery. The grounds are kept attractive by a small army of robotic gardening devices. The company uses the grounds as a test facility for its landscaping division. As we walked through the front door we were greeted by a pretty woman in a bright yellow dress. As she welcomed us, we noticed that her voice sounded strange. We suddenly realized that she was a robot.

Bobbie did a ton of research on Jenny Bateman, as she always does with a new matter. A lot of people still believe that Jenny was the person who killed the jihadis who assassinated her husband. If I were a betting man, I'd wager that Jenny was the killer, based on Bobbie's research. But that isn't the case we're assigned to. Our job is to find out as much as we can about the aerial drones.

A robotic assistant escorted us into Jenny Bateman's office. It was a three-foot high orange robot on wheels. The machine greeted us in a perfectly clear voice and said, "Welcome to Robot Depot. My name is Jake and I'll show you into our president's office." We thanked Jake. It felt weird to be thanking a machine, but hey, this is Robot Depot.

The office was large, as you would expect for the office of the CEO of a big company. Placed around the office was every type of robotic device you could imagine, from floor cleaners to window washers to greeters.

Jenny Bateman is a strikingly pretty woman with light blue eyes, in her early 40s according to Bobbie's research. She wore her brunette hair shoulder length. To get off on the right foot, I wanted to get something out of the way.

"Ms. Bateman…"

"Please call me Jenny. Is it okay if I call you Bob and Bobbie? I've read a lot about you two."

As we had heard, Jenny Bateman is a charming, friendly person.

"I just want to be clear about something, Jenny. This interview has nothing to do with the assassination of those terrorists that a lot of people speculate may have involved you."

"Oh yes, those poor dears. I just hope they didn't suffer too much," she said with a chuckle and a smirk.

I almost cracked up. I got the impression that Jenny Bateman isn't a woman who takes shit from anybody. "Good for her," as Ralph said, "the scumbags had it coming." An old phrase I love is that the enemy of our enemy is our friend. That would make Jenny our friend.

"I'm sure you guys want to talk about those drones that were used in that disgusting attack on a high school football game."

"Yes, we're trying to find out everything about them," I said.

"Phil," she yelled into her intercom to her assistant, "bring in one of those X253s please."

In walked Phil, holding a small drone aircraft. Phil was a well-dressed man, about 5'11." His hair looked like it was just done up in a salon. Phil placed the drone on Jenny's desk and turned to leave the room.

"Stick around, Phil. I want you to help me answer questions," Jenny said. Phil responded in a strange voice that sounded like it came from another part of the room. Bobbie tapped my arm and looked at me wide-eyed. Holy shit, Phil was a robot.

Jenny grabbed a remote and pressed a button. The drone took off as she guided its flight with her remote. It buzzed like a bee, just as we've heard from witnesses at the stadium. She navigated it around the room with her small remote. I was amazed at the way the drone responded to her finger touches. She pressed another button and the buzzing noise stopped. The drone was now soundless.

"I'm surprised that you can turn off the sound," I said. "You would think that the terrorists who used the drones would silence them, but from the reports we've heard, they were all in buzz mode when the attack occurred."

"I'm guessing that they leave the sound turned on to add to the terror," Jenny said. "Terrorists are horrible people, the scum of the earth. I'm glad I…"

My guess is that Jenny wanted to say, "I'm glad I killed the bastards." But she just let her voice trail off.

"What are these things usually used for?" Bobbie asked.

"Aerial reconnaissance is the primary use intended. The NYPD is a big customer of ours."

Phil just stood there, smiling all the while. When he moved his head, I noticed a slight whirring sound.

"But in the hands of the wrong person, they can deliver explosives, yes?" I said.

"Yes, and that's why I've lobbied till I'm blue in the face that these things should be controlled, more so even than guns," Jenny said. "That would cut down on our market a bit, but fuck it, there's more to life than Robot Depot profits."

It's easy to like this lady.

"Flat out question, Jenny," Bobbie said, "have there been any major purchases of these things, not to mention thefts?"

"We always get large orders for drones, but we're sure there have been no thefts, not from Robot Depot anyway. The FBI has been all over this as of this morning. We have an extremely strict method of tracking inventory, put in place by my late husband. But once they're turned loose in the market, anybody can accumulate a lot of them, tamper with them and raise hell, as we saw yesterday. That's why I keep insisting on better government controls." I noticed her wipe away a tear when she mentioned her late husband. From what I've read about the Batemans they were as close as Bobbie and me.

I couldn't get over how straight she was with us. This lady, the CEO of a huge company, actually wants more regulating of her products. Jenny Bateman is the real deal.

"I notice the book that you wrote, *Robot Depot*, on the shelf behind you," Bobbie said. "Can we buy a signed copy from you?"

"It's my gift to law enforcement. Just make sure you give it a review on Amazon." She reached behind her, grabbed the book, and signed it.

The inscription above her signature read, "To my friends, the BBs."

Jenny and Phil then went into detail on how this X253 works, how it's launched, and more important, how it's guided.

"Are you sure this is the drone that was used at the stadium attack?" Bobbie asked.

"Yes. One of the FBI guys brought in one that hadn't exploded. It's definitely an X253. A small bomb was attached to it, which turned out to be a dud."

"Jenny, is Robot Depot able to place a tracking device on its drones?" I said.

"Wow, I've read that you two are sharp detectives and you just proved it. Yes, it's something we're working on as a long-term project."

"May I make a recommendation?" Bobbie said.

"When one of the famous BBs makes a recommendation, I'm all ears."

"I suggest that you accelerate that drone tracking project."

"Consider it done, Bobbie. Phil, make a note of that and get me an appointment with our engineering manager."

Phil nodded and walked out the door.

"Jenny, you've been most helpful. We may need to talk to you again," Bobbie said.

"Sure, and here's my cellphone number. Call me with any questions at all. My fucking products are killing people and I want to stop it as much as you do."

Bobbie and I agreed that we had made a new friend.

CHAPTER 22

A li Mussin had just placed a bag against a strut under the control booth at MetLife Stadium in East Rutherford, New Jersey. He had been doing the same thing for two weeks. He was hired a month ago as a porter, a general handyman. He looked at a piece of paper, making sure that he had placed bags at all the intended locations. His work done, he went to his locker and changed from his uniform into jeans and a sweatshirt. In the past two weeks he had placed 75 bags in selected locations. He walked out of the stadium at 6:30.

The Monday night game between the New York Giants and the New York Jets would begin at 8:20 p.m. to a capacity crowd of 82,500 people. The Giants-Jets game is one of the most popular in the NFL.

As he walked to his car, Ali realized that he had one remaining bag in his coat pocket. He walked back into the stadium. No way did he have time to place the bag in the selected location, so he just placed it next to a food stand on the first level. It wasn't on his list, but he knew it would make a great target.

The bag, as all the other bags, contained Pentaerythritol

tetranitrate, or PETN, the prime ingredient of Semtex, one of the most powerful explosives known to science.

—————————

The Giants won the toss and elected to receive. The kickoff was returned by safety Jabrill Peppers to the Jets' 30-yard line. Quarterback Eli Manning lined up behind the center for the snap. He heard a loud buzzing sound as if a swarm of bees surrounded the field. Because of the distraction, Manning motioned to the referee, signaling for a time out. He looked up and saw a flight of aerial drones heading to various spots in the stadium. His trained eye estimated there were over 100 of the small aircraft.

The first five drones crashed into the broadcast booth, which had been heavily packed with bags of Semtex. Each of the drones exploded, causing the Semtex-laden bags to detonate. The resulting blast shook the stadium. The broadcast booth came loose from its fittings, teetered for a moment, and plummeted onto the spectators in the seats below. Ninety-five people died, crushed under the multi-ton broadcast booth. The next group of drones dove toward selected spots on the huge scoreboard, causing it to fall forward from the gigantic explosions.

A primary target for the drones was the lighting structure that surrounded the stadium at its highest level, a sort of narrow roof with spotlights. The base of each supporting beam was packed with bags of Semtex. A large group of drones hovered over the field, and, on signal, dove straight for the supporting beams simultaneously. Robbed of its support beams, the entire structure fell on top of the people below, killing hundreds.

The football players, now spectators themselves to the scene of mass destruction, stayed on the field as they watched the stadium around them being destroyed.

At 8:35 p.m., 15 minutes after the kickoff, the explosions stopped. 15,438 people lay dead, many of whom were crushed in the stampede to evacuate the stadium. Hundreds more were seriously wounded. The night air was pierced by the screams of the dying and wounded, the wailing of sirens, and the sounds of medivac helicopters swarming onto the field.

CHAPTER 23

Bobbie

B ob and I walked into Federal Plaza on Tuesday morning, a short distance from One PP. FBI Director Sarah Watson was in town and asked to meet us. We met in the office of Rick Bellamy, Secretary of Homeland Security. We know both Sarah and Rick well, and I couldn't help but notice that they both had a funereal look about them. Sarah normally jumps up to meet us, and Rick always smiles and puts out his hand. But neither of them moved, merely nodding their heads as a greeting. I guess Bob and I looked somber too. The attack on MetLife Stadium last night hung over the room like a pallor. Although there were three large windows in Rick's office, a heavy cloud cover added to the bleak atmosphere.

"I spoke to Commissioner Norquist about this," Sarah said, "and he readily agreed. I'm once again appointing you two as provisional FBI agents and putting you in charge of investigating last night's horror. Because it happened in New Jersey, you can't head up the investigation as NYPD detectives."

Then she broke down in tears, sobbing, trying to find her voice.

"My brother and sister-in-law were at the game," she said, her voice choking. "They're both dead, along with more than 15,000 other people." She blew her nose. "I'm sorry for acting like this, but I'm sure you understand."

I walked over to Sarah's chair, leaned over, kissed her on the cheek, and held her hand.

"I'm seldom at a loss for words, Sarah, but all I can say is I'm terribly sorry."

"We'll find these bastards, Sarah," Bob said. "I promise you we will."

"From the FBI's preliminary investigation last night," Rick Bellamy said, "we believe that quantities of Semtex had been placed throughout the stadium, and the drones dove straight at those locations. This was a carefully orchestrated attack by some sophisticated terrorists."

"Bob and I met with Jenny Bateman, CEO of Robot Depot, yesterday afternoon after the attack on the high school football game the day before. We know that the drones were manufactured by Robot Depot, and Jenny Bateman has promised total cooperation with our investigation. She's one sharp lady. She's stopped manufacturing the drones until this case is solved, but that isn't much help because there are thousands of them already out there in the market."

"Rick, you said that the FBI has discovered traces of Semtex, which explains the gigantic explosions," Bob said. "The Semtex was obviously put there by a person or a group. The first thing we want to look at is the personnel records of employees."

"For once, we're ahead of you guys," Rick said. "This morning we received a database from stadium management with all of the employees' records. Have at it, guys; they're all yours."

"I think we should go public and ask for any indication of where the drones launched," I said. "The only problem is that they were helicopter drones and could have been launched from multiple locations without the need for a runway. The communications technology is advanced from what we know, and the drones can be controlled from a long distance. We'll want to ask Jenny Bateman of Robot Depot for more detail on that."

"Bob and I will go now to the stadium and start asking questions. What do you think, Bob?"

"Yes, let's go there now. We should turn loose Joyce Randolph and tell her to start combing through the personnel records. Joyce is amazing at sorting through data."

"This Thursday night the Eagles are playing the Dolphins at Lincoln Financial Field in Philadelphia," Rick said. "I'm not paid to think negatively, but I'm concerned."

"I don't think anything will happen, Rick," Sarah said, still looking grim. "Whoever is doing this must know that the stadium will be under maximum security. I'm going to order two helicopters to be in the air over the stadium at all times. The FBI will bill the NFL for the copters. I already spoke to the NFL Commissioner about that. No drone will be able to get near the place."

"But you don't need a drone to detonate a bag of Semtex," I said. They all looked at me as if they wished I hadn't said that.

CHAPTER 24

Bob

Our FBI driver took Bobbie and me to MetLife Stadium in East Rutherford, New Jersey, about a 35-minute drive. On the way we called Jane, our babysitter, and asked to speak to Tilly. "Hi Daddy, hi Mommy," she said. That little beauty has wrapped her arms around our hearts.

As we pulled away from Federal Plaza, my phone sounded. It was Joyce Randolph, our diligent research assistant. I put it on speaker so Bobbie could hear.

"I haven't gone through the entire list of names, but I figured I should alert you to one guy I found. His name is Ali Mussin and he's on both the CIA and FBI watch lists. He works as a porter, a sort of general handyman, at MetLife Stadium. He began the job a month ago. According to the watch lists, he's been implicated in bombings using Semtex."

"Great work as usual, Joyce. Get a search warrant for his residence and let us know when it's been executed. Let us know if you find anybody else."

Bobbie and I looked at each other. A MetLife Stadium employee who's on the watch lists and is suspected of bombings using Semtex. God bless Joyce Randolph.

Because our car bore an FBI insignia, we were able to get through the barricades. The place looked more like a battlefield than a football stadium. From a large opening in one of the stadium walls we could see the field. The viewing stands were strewn with large pieces of debris. Huge sections of seats were no longer there. Bomb sniffing dogs patrolled the stands, led by their handlers. Teams of paramedics carried more stretchers than I could count, stretchers covered with body bags. The main entrance was a pile of rubble and was surrounded by crime scene tape, so we circled around and walked through a door marked "Deliveries." We wore black vests with the huge white FBI letters on front and back, which Bobbie thought was totally cool.

When the cop at the door let us in, I immediately noticed the odor of Semtex, combined with the smell of smoke, and yes, the smell of death. Not pleasant aromas. We went to the office of George Mason, the general manager of the stadium, who had been alerted that we were coming. We walked down a long corridor and noticed that the area had not been hit by explosives, but you wouldn't know it from the odor.

His assistant showed us into his office. The office walls were adorned with posters of each team in the NFL. The posters for the Giants and Jets, the teams that share MetLife stadium as their homefield, were larger than the others and were centered on the wall. From Bobbie's research—Bobbie always does research on an interrogee—Mason was 45 years old and was 5'10" tall. He graduated from NYU and had been employed by the NFL for all his working career. The guy we saw looked like he should be in a hospital. His left arm was in a sling, and he wore a large bandage on his forehead. He motioned us to two chairs in front of his desk. He told us to call him George and asked us to speak loudly because his ears were still ringing.

"I'm glad to see that the FBI works fast. You two look familiar. I think I've seen your pictures in newspapers and on TV."

"We're detectives with the NYPD, but we're also provisional agents with the FBI," I said.

"Oh my God, you're the famous BBs. I'm happy to see that the government is taking this case seriously. Whatever I can do to help, just let me know."

He winced in pain and gently touched the bandage on his head.

He told us, detail by detail from his recollection, about the night of horror. We were shocked when he told us that he had just left the control booth a minute before it exploded, narrowly avoiding death.

"We have a question about one of your employees, George. Do you personally know a man named Ali Mussin?"

"Yeah, we hired him about a month ago as a porter, a sort of handyman to do odd jobs. Hey, wait a minute, I just realized something. Yesterday, about two hours before game time the guy disappeared. I was pissed off because I had an assignment for him to handle. But he simply wasn't here."

Mason walked over to a file cabinet and retrieved the folder about Ali Mussin. I didn't tell him that we already had an electronic copy of all employee records at the NYPD. People often get squeamish when they know that you have information about them. Apparently, the FBI got the records from another manager. He opened the file and told us the guy lived in East Rutherford, not far from the stadium. Of course, we already knew that and had told Joyce to get a search warrant for his apartment.

"Did you have any disciplinary issues with him?" Bobbie asked.

"He had a problem showing up at the right time. He was often seen wandering around the stadium for no apparent reason. After last night, I think I'm going to fire his ass."

"Are you sure you'll see him again?" I asked.

"What do you mean?"

"What if I told you that he's on both the CIA and FBI watch lists. He's a suspect in a couple of bombings involving Semtex, the explosive that was used here last night."

"Holy shit! Do you think this guy may have had something to do with last night?"

"It's a theory we're working on," I said.

"You would have thought that I'd know about the guy's background. We're pretty careful about who we hire."

"Well, I wouldn't expect that his possible terrorist activities would wind up on a resume," Bobbie said.

Bobbie and I looked at each other and had one of our non-verbal communications.

"George, thank you for your assistance. I'm sure we'll be talking again soon."

As we walked out of the stadium, my phone sounded. It was Joyce Randolph.

"I got the search warrant, Bob. Because it's in another state we couldn't have NYPD officers execute it. Commissioner Ralph contacted FBI Director Watson who got an FBI warrant. She personally hustled it through. Two agents and a federal marshal are on their way there now. Here's the address."

We had our driver take us to 235 Ninth Street, East Rutherford, New Jersey, the address of the mysterious Mr. Ali Mussin. The FBI guys and the federal marshal met us at the front door. We rang the bell, and as we expected, got no answer. The marshal broke the door open with a battering ram, a useful piece of equipment when executing a search warrant. The apartment was neat and didn't appear to have been occupied recently. I immediately noticed a group of bags lined up next to the living room wall. I didn't want to touch the bags, as I suspected what was in them. I kneeled and sniffed. Semtex. The four of us walked room to room, which didn't take long because it was only a three-room apartment. The walls were decked with radical jihadi posters, a few of which called for "Death to America." I called the bomb squad to retrieve the Semtex. Those people know how to handle dangerous explosives. Bobbie and I dusted every surface for fingerprints. All five of us wore latex gloves, of course. We noticed very few articles of clothing. Seems like the place may have been vacated in a hurry.

"Hey, Bob, check out this poster," Bobbie said. It bore an interesting message.

"Infidels love to frolic in their sports stadiums and watch their heathen games. That will soon end." Under those words was a sketch of a football stadium erupting in flames.

"Seems like we've got our guy, Bob."

"Yeah, but where the hell *is* he?"

CHAPTER 25

Bobbie

Bob and I walked to Federal Plaza where we'd meet with Sarah Watson, Rick Bellamy, and Ralph Norquist.

After we searched Ali Mussin's apartment, Bob and I felt confident that we had the identity of our guy, or at least one of them. Problem is, he seems to have fled in a hurry, even leaving behind bags of Semtex. On Joyce Randolph's suggestion, Ralph had put out an APB (All-Points Bulletin) on Ali Mussin, along with a photograph from his personnel file.

We told them about our meeting with the manager of MetLife Stadium, as well as the details of our search of Mussin's apartment. I showed them a photo of the poster that talked about frolicking infidels, the one with the sketch of the exploding stadium. They went silent, as if they just discovered something that couldn't be denied. It was him.

"That APB was a heads-up idea, Ralph," Sarah said, "but from what Bob and Bobbie tell us, the man was last seen at about 6:30 last night. He could be half-way around the world by now."

My phone rang. "It's Joyce," I said. "I better take the call."

I put her on speaker.

"Sometimes things go the way we want them to," Joyce said in a loud voice. "We nailed Ali Mussin at JFK as he was about to board a flight to Saudi Arabia. He's in custody and is on his way to Federal Plaza now."

We all exchange high-fives. It's that wonderful breakthrough feeling that law enforcement people get when something opens up. Our "suspect" is on his way.

About a half-hour later a cop was escorted into the office by Rick's assistant. He didn't look happy.

"Your suspect is dead, folks. On our way here he popped a couple of pills, killing himself. According to the doctor from the medical department downstairs, it was cyanide. We had searched him, of course, but pills are easy to conceal."

"Back to square one" is a phrase that all detectives hate. But that's exactly where Bob and I found ourselves, back to square one. We had our primary suspect, Ali Mussin, but we were sure there were a lot of people besides him, specifically the people who operated the drones.

But how to find them?

CHAPTER 26

Bobbie

Bob and I make it a point not to worry. Just get the job done and don't waste time worrying. But we *were* worried. Death from above caused by a small object that looks like a toy is our new reality.

So, although it was against our grain, Bob and I were worried as hell.

We try not to wear pickle pusses when we're around little Tilly. It isn't hard, because Tilly makes us smile whether we feel like it or not.

I suddenly remembered that my cousin Grace Blakely, with whom I constantly chat with by email and text, said that she, her husband Frank, and their two teenage sons would attend the Eagles-Dolphins game. They live in Philadelphia and have season tickets to Eagles home games. I texted her: "Don't even fucking think about going to that game tonight. Remember MetLife Stadium?" God, I hope she listens to me. Grace and Frank have a reputation for acting impulsively. A few minutes later, Grace texted back: "Read you loud and clear, Bobbie. We'll skip the game. If nothing happens, you owe me a martini."

Six men, dressed in the uniforms of NFL officials, patrolled Lincoln Financial Field two hours before game time scheduled for 8:20. Nothing unusual. Each man carried a small satchel over his shoulder. Also, nothing unusual. It was normal for patrolling officials to pick up debris from the field and place it in their bags so that the field would be neat and clean by game time. The men looked up and saw two FBI helicopters patrolling the sky over the stadium. They laughed. Inside each of their satchels were 10 small 4" by 4" helicopter drones. They placed drones at the edge of the field 50 feet apart. The tiny crafts weren't visible to the naked eye unless you were right on top of them. It was now 7:40, a half-hour to the kickoff.

Philadelphia won the toss and the Eagles elected to receive. DeAndre Carter caught the kickoff and returned the ball to the Dolphins 45-yard line. Eagles quarterback Nick Foles took the snap and fell back for a play action pass, faking a handoff to running back Josh Adams. Foles threw downfield to Joshua Perkins, who caught the ball for a 12-yard gain. As he walked back to the huddle, Foles glanced up and was happy to see two FBI helicopters hovering over the stadium. That should keep any exploding drones away, he thought. He called a running play and the Eagles clapped their hands and jogged to the line of scrimmage. He was about to call the count when he heard a loud buzzing sound coming from the walls of the stadium. Players for both teams looked around to try to identify the sound. Realizing that the attention was lost, Foles called for a time out.

The 60 drones flew to their assigned locations. The first one hit just below the broadcast booth, and the Semtex bag exploded along with the drone. The booth teetered lopsided, looking like it was about to fall. It did, two minutes later, after four more drones hit, crushing hundreds of spectators below.

Four drones smashed into the main gate, causing it to collapse, aided by the implanted Semtex bags. The main gate is the location most of the spectators would use to exit the stadium.

The Skycam, which is actually a flying drone, gives the viewers a comprehensive view of the playing field below. The planners of the attack didn't target the Skycam, because they wanted the TV audience to view the carnage below.

Tim and Marilyn McLaughlin had just returned from their honeymoon in Cancun the day before the game. Tim's father had given them tickets to the game as one of his wedding presents. Both Tim and Marilyn are die-hard Eagles fans and were delighted with their gift. Tim, a former running back with the University of Oklahoma, had a try-out with the Eagles the year before, although he didn't make the final cut. They sat, munching hot dogs, and perused the list of players and the stats from previous games. "What's that noise?" Tim said.

In the final moment of their lives, they looked up in shock as a drone dived toward them and exploded two feet over their heads.

Even though Lincoln Financial Field had a capacity of 69,696, just over 15,000 were in attendance that day, largely due to the lingering doubts about the disaster at MetLife Stadium just days before. In this evening's attack, 9,429 people lost their lives in the explosions. Area hospitals were stressed to their limits with wounded patients. FEMA dispatched helicopters with field hospital equipment.

My cousin, Grace, texted me. "Looks like I owe *you* a martini. God bless you, cousin Bobbie."

CHAPTER 27

Wolf Blitzer for *CNN*, ladies and gentlemen. For the past week there is only one story to report, a story of unmitigated horror. It began a few days ago with an attack by exploding helicopter drones on Memorial Field in Flushing, where over 600 people lost their lives in the sickening attack on a high school football game. That was followed up the next evening with an attack on MetLife Stadium, where the New York Giants played the New York Jets. The drones in that attack targeted pre-packaged bags of the highly explosive Semtex, ensuring a maximum loss of life. A capacity crowd of over 80,000 was gathered to watch the big game. It saddens me to say that 15,438 people lost their lives.

"Three days later, last night, we saw an attack on Lincoln Financial Field in Philadelphia where the Philadelphia Eagles had just received the kickoff from the Miami Dolphins. The crowd was thinner than expected because of the lingering horror of the attack on MetLife Stadium just days before. Despite the poor attendance, no fewer than 9,429 people were killed. Sarah Watson, the Director of the FBI, had ordered helicopters to hover over the stadium, but it was later discovered that at least 60 helicopter drones loaded with explosives were placed along the edges of the field. The circling helicopter pilots never saw them. Just as with the MetLife Stadium attack, last night's disaster also saw the use of Semtex, a highly explosive substance. You may recall that a small bag of Semtex was detonated and brought down a 747 over Lockerbie, Scotland a few years back. The bags of Semtex were placed at carefully chosen targets in the stadium to ensure maximum casualties.

"We have with us on the line, Rick Bellamy, Secretary of Homeland Security. Secretary Bellamy will fill us in on the latest efforts to forestall these disasters. Welcome to *CNN*, Mr. Secretary."

"Good evening, Wolf. I'm glad that I have the opportunity to advise your viewers what is being done to forestall the horrible attacks on athletic stadiums. In consultation with the NFL, the NCAA, the FBI, as well as police chiefs across the nation, we have developed a new set of security protocols for football games. These protocols are intended to accomplish one thing: to save lives. Before any game, bomb-sniffing dogs will roam a stadium to detect any placements of Semtex or other explosives. There will be a minimum of two helicopters hovering over every game, although that did not prevent the scene at Lincoln Financial Field in Philadelphia because the drones that targeted the Semtex were launched from ground level at the stadium. To prevent that from occurring, squads of police officers will scour the field and seating areas before every game, along with the dogs. We are also seeing to it that high intensity radar be installed at every stadium to detect an approaching flight of drones.

"Government cost, at the federal, state, and local level, will be shared by the organization hosting the game, such as the National Football League. Because of the enormous cost of these measures, high schools and small colleges have a particular problem. My office has been tracking this crisis, and, I'm sad to say that 85 percent of high school football programs have been cancelled as of yesterday, as well as 75 percent of small college programs. The terrorists who are making this happen are having a gigantic impact on American culture in just a few days.

"We feel confident that these measures will help stave off future attacks. But I warn you, when dealing with terrorism, nothing is guaranteed. And have no doubt about it, these actions are terrorism, the worst form of terrorism we can imagine."

"Thank you, Secretary Bellamy, for your expert analysis of this crisis and especially for you comforting words about what is being done to prevent future incidents. Good night, sir.

"In other news…"

CHAPTER 28

Bob

Bobbie and I met again with Jenny Bateman, CEO of Robot Depot, the manufacturer of the drones of terror. She requested the meeting and came to our temporary FBI office at Federal Plaza. We were about to call Jenny anyway after our meeting with Rick Bellamy and Sarah Watson. We invited Rick Bellamy and Commissioner Ralph to sit in on the meeting. Sarah Watson was in California that day.

Jenny was accompanied by a man we hadn't met before. His name was Liam Jackson but everybody at Robot Depot calls him "Billy" after the character in the 1982 movie, *Computers are People Too*. Billy dragged behind him a suitcase on wheels. I wondered what was in the suitcase. Maybe he's planning to catch a flight after our meeting. When she introduced us, Jenny said that Billy is the Vice President of Science and Research at Robot Depot.

Bobbie and I have taken a liking to Jenny. She isn't your typical CEO who spends all her time watching her company's stock price. She's a patriot and she gets it. As she told us the first time we met with her: "My fucking products are killing people and I want to stop it as much as you."

I was surprised to see that Jenny and Rick Bellamy knew each other well. They even hugged. Bellamy would later tell me that the last time her company's products were used by terrorist, she worked closely with Rick at Homeland Security and Sarah Watson with the FBI. She wrote about it extensively in her book, *Robot Depot*. I'm still convinced that she killed the terrorists who assassinated her husband, but I don't care. You go, girl.

Rick shook hands with Billy, obviously knowing him.

Then Rick turned to the suitcase and said, "Good morning, Angus."

"Good morning, Secretary Bellamy," the suitcase said.

Bobbie and I just stared at each other. This will be an interesting meeting.

"Something tells me that the geniuses at Robot Depot have come up with some good ideas," Rick Bellamy said.

"Yes, we have, Rick, and I think you'll like it. I told Bob and Bobbie about a major project we've been working on to track drones in flight. At Bobbie's urging, I fast-tracked the plans. They're two sharp detectives and know how to drive home a point. Bottom line, we've developed a device that can not only track our drones but can disable them in flight. It's a system we've been working on with a United States Army contract. What I just said is top secret, but fuck it, we need to put this show on the road."

Jenny is charmingly blunt in her use of language.

"Can this tracking technology be used with existing drones or only new ones?" Bobbie asked. I'm constantly amazed at Bobbie's grasp of technology.

"As I told you the last time we met, we've stopped manufacturing the drones because of the recent attacks. But now we're ready to start up again. The new drones will now include a tracking device. With the older drones that are already on the market, we can track them as well, but not as efficiently. Each drone, including the older ones, has an electronic signature that enables us to locate it. It's a simple matter of installing a *Drone Tracker*, as we call it, on a structure, say a football stadium. Once the Tracker locks in, we're able to disable the drone. The signal also disables the triggering mechanism for a drone-mounted bomb."

"Holy shit," the four of us said. Sometimes the perfect words announce themselves when you've heard something shocking.

"The Drone Tracker was developed by Angus here," Jenny said, gesturing toward the suitcase. "I'm sorry I haven't introduced Angus formally. He was invented by Billy. Angus is the world's first sentient robot, meaning that it's aware of its own existence, just like human beings. Billy is working on a humanoid appearance for Angus, so he doesn't need to drag him around in a suitcase."

"I do hope you mean human, not humanoid, Jenny," the suitcase said. I had never seen a suitcase object to being insulted. "Ayooga, ayooga, ayooga," Angus said. I guessed that's what a robot sounds like when it laughs.

"Is this *Drone Track*er very expensive?" Rick asked, his eyes wide as frisbees.

"Although the programming is highly sophisticated, the material costs aren't high. Our cost, including development, to manufacture a *Drone Tracker* is $3,500. I'm perfectly willing to provide them to the government at our cost. I've already cleared this with my board of directors. We expect to make a fortune with our Army contract, so we're only too happy to help out with this stadium attacking shit. Please ignore what I just said about making a fortune off the Army."

"Is it complicated to install these devices?" I asked.

"No, Bob. All you need is a few bolts and an electric outlet and you're good to go. If an electric outlet isn't available, you can use battery power."

"When can we start?" Ralph Norquist asked. Ralph likes to move things along, as I've always noticed.

"I figured you guys want to move fast, so I had one of my company trucks follow me here. It's in your parking lot. It contains 75 *Drone Trackers*, and more will be available as needed.

"I've said it before, and I'll say it again," Rick said. "You are one great American, Jenny Bateman. Thank you."

"You can thank Detectives Bob and Bobbie here. They're the ones who lit a candle under my ass."

CHAPTER 29

Bobbie

After our meeting with Jenny Bateman at Rick Bellamy's office, I'm feeling a bit more confident that we may have this crap on the run. With the new security protocols that Rick has announced, it's unlikely that somebody can pull off a Semtex bombing without drone help. Jenny's amazing *Drone Tracker* to the rescue. She's definitely on my *favorite people* list.

Bob and I are still working out of Federal Plaza, much to Commissioner Ralph's chagrin. He prefers us at One Police Plaza, and we agree with him. We think of ourselves as cops, not federal agents, but recent events have required us to be FBI agents again. Bob and I were in Rick Bellamy's office and are about to meet with our old friend, Buster, aka Charles Atkins, Director of the Central Intelligence Agency.

We've worked many a case with Buster and his people. He even awarded us provisional CIA agent status. Buster is a tall, good-looking man at 6'1." His parents are Coptic Christians from Egypt, and Buster's appearance shows his Middle Eastern lineage. He speaks fluent Arabic. Buster jokingly calls himself a jihadi's worst nightmare, but it's no joke as Bob and I have witnessed on many occasions. He insists that people call him Buster, even subordinates.

"Director Atkins, I mean Buster, is here for his meeting," Rick's assistant said.

Buster walked in and gave us both bear hugs. We think of him as one of our best friends.

"So, no surprise that you guys nailed it by finding that bastard Ali Mussin, although he killed himself before you could interrogate him. He saved me the trouble of killing him. Forget what I just said, okay?"

"Because we suspect that the leadership of this stadium attack operation is from the Middle East, I guess you have your moles all over the ground," I said.

"I can't confirm that, Bobbie."

"You just did," I said, laughing. Buster cracked up. He knows he can't bullshit me.

"The Army-Navy Game is next week," Buster said. "President Fenton, a Naval Academy grad, put out the word to me as well as FBI Director Watson, that he doesn't want to see America's most popular game turned into a scene of mass murder. Your thoughts on that, BBs?"

I told Buster about Robot Depot's *Drone Tracker*, which I was sure he'd learn about soon anyway.

"With the *Drone Trackers* and the new security protocols for all games, Bob and I are convinced that this show is over. Any terrorist activity at a football stadium will be a small affair, nothing like we've seen. God knows, it's taken a toll. High schools and small colleges simply can't afford the security protocols."

The intercom buzzed.

"Go ahead, Nancy," Rick said to his assistant.

"I'm sorry to interrupt, but I just got a heads-up from a TV producer about something I think you'll be interested in. Turn on your TV and tune to *Fox News*."

"Martha McCallum for *Fox News*, ladies and gentlemen. Our city and our nation are still recovering from the horrific attacks on football stadiums in the past few weeks. But with new technology and enhanced security measures, we believe the danger is over. But big problems persist for high schools and small colleges, most of which have cancelled their football programs because of the high cost of security. Well, for high schools on Long Island, the problem has been taken care of. None other than Robot Depot, the labor-saving device giant, has come forward with an announcement that it will cover the $50,000 per season security cost for each of the 656 high schools in Nassau and Suffolk counties. That comes out to almost $33 million. You will recall that the horrible exploding drone helicopters that caused so much disaster were manufactured by Robot Depot. The company wasn't implicated in any way, and even used its sophisticated technology to disable drones in flight. Robot Depot CEO Jennifer Bateman, whom everybody calls Jenny, made the announcement this morning. Hats off to a great American company that's willing to step up to the plate. Expect to see the public relations committees of other American corporations follow suit."

"Have I mentioned that Jenny Bateman is on my *favorite people list*," I said.

CHAPTER 30

Bob

Bobbie and I were in our office preparing for our next case.

"So, now that the stadium attacks are basically handled, what should we work on?" Bobbie said.

"I have two words for you—East Hampton."

"Yesss," she screamed and ran around to my side of the desk. She threw her arms around me and squeezed. Safe to say that Bobbie likes going to our house in East Hampton as much as I do. It was Thursday morning, so I figured we'd take off Friday and Monday for some R&R. Commissioner Ralph readily agreed. We went to our apartment to pick up Jane and Tilly. Jane's fiancé, Steve Rankin, will join us on Saturday.

I drove our rented car to John Reynolds Café, one of our favorite lunch places in East Hampton. Sal, our friend and waiter seated us. Jane was back at the house with Tilly. She wanted to show Tilly how to play checkers. She then wants to teach her to play chess—Jane, the babysitter sent from God.

"There's somebody I'd like you to meet," Sal said. "Say Hi to Evelyn Reynolds, the owner of the John Reynolds Café."

A well-dressed woman, I figured she was about 55 or so, reached out her hand to us. She was tall and quite pretty.

"Wow, it's an honor to meet you two. I've heard nothing but great things about you. I'm delighted that you picked my place for lunch. We don't often get to serve law enforcement celebrities."

We asked her to join us, and she seemed happy to agree.

"My late husband loved this place. When I inherited it, I wasn't sure I wanted to take over, but I'm glad I did. It's a joy, especially meeting great folks like you."

Her phone beeped. "Sorry, I have to take this."

"Anything new, Commissioner?" She said.

We couldn't follow the conversation because the phone wasn't on speaker, not that we wanted to eavesdrop anyway. She didn't seem happy with what the man was saying. I wondered what he was commissioner of.

When she hung up, she looked completely distraught. Her smile had been replaced by a grimace.

"Everything okay?" I said, mainly to be polite in the awkward silence.

"I'm really sorry to be acting like this as you two are out here trying to enjoy yourselves. That was Mike Townsend, Suffolk County Police Commissioner."

"Bobbie and I know Mike well. We've had him and his wife to dinner at our place."

"Yes, Commissioner Mike is a good guy," Evelyn said, "but even he's stumped by this case. My Mom, at age 82, was defrauded by what is best described as an Internet con man. She lost $300,000, her life savings. She also lost her house when the bank foreclosed. She now lives with me. This shit happened only last year, and it's been hell."

"Dear Lord," Bobbie said. "What happened, if you don't mind me asking."

"When one of the best detectives in the country asks me a question, I'm only too happy to answer you. My mom doesn't suffer from senility, but, like a lot of elderly people, she has a habit of being too trusting. She loves her computer and the Internet and spends most of her day online. She got a call one day from guy saying that he was from Microsoft and wanted to warn her that her computer was in danger because it had been infected by a virus. He said that to kill the virus, mom would need to let him log in to her system."

"Oh shit," I said.

"Yeah, oh shit indeed. So, trusting Mom gave him her login credentials. He then asked if she uses QuickBooks accounting software. Mom, a former bookkeeper, said yes. The caller said the virus in question often originates in QuickBooks so he would need her password to the software so he could check. Her screen then went blank. The guy explained that it was normal during a virus check. You can't make this shit up. So, still not suspecting anything, mom just sat there as the guy raided her files. A week later her savings were gone. She couldn't afford the mortgage payment without her savings, so the bank foreclosed."

"It happened that fast?" Bobbie said.

"No, it didn't. Mom was embarrassed so she never told me about the incident—until the bank foreclosed six months later. I could have easily covered her mortgage payments, but I had no idea what was happening. By then, any possibility of finding the scammer was gone. I asked mom if she could check back on her cellphone messages. She found the number, remembering the day it happened. I called the number and got the message: 'The number you are trying to reach is no longer in service.' I did some research about cyber scams and I was shocked to see that it's a common problem, especially among senior citizens. It's as if they're rabbits living next to a wolf den."

"Bobbie and I are fond of elderly people, probably because we both have terrific grandparents. We even volunteer to help at a nearby senior center. The big problem, as you just told us, is with elderly people living alone, without senior care management to look after them."

"So, from your disappointing conversation with Mike Townsend, it sounds like your mom is out of luck." Bobbie said.

"Yes, flat out of luck. The thief stole away into the night leaving no footprints. Hey, I must run along for a dentist appointment. My conversation with Mike Townsend took up a lot of time. Lunch is on me."

We insisted that we pay for lunch, but Evelyn wouldn't hear of it.

"Evelyn, here's my business card. Call me if you think I may be helpful, but frankly I'm not sure what Bobbie or I can do."

When we got to our house, we both hugged Tilly, and Bobbie immediately sat in front of one of our computers. I could tell Bobbie wanted to dive into research, and when she wants to find out information, nobody is faster than her, especially when she's pissed off. I was angry myself. The story Evelyn Reynolds told us was sickening. A defenseless old lady ripped off by an Internet con artist. I sat at the workstation next to Bobbie's. After about an hour of research, we were both floored. We researched stories of elderly people being conned out of their money. The problem was bigger than we imagined. We then concentrated on cases in New York City, cases over which Bobbie and I can have jurisdiction. I know what we're going to talk to Commissioner Ralph about when we get back. We normally take cases as they're assigned to us, but Bobbie and I agreed that we would prepare a sales pitch for Ralph to turn us loose on this shit.

Bobbie stood and stretched. She often gets stiff when she's working on something while she's angry.

"Hey, Bob, you know what time it is?"

"According to the clock on the wall, it's 5:45."

"No, it's hot tub time. We'll work on this Internet con job case when we get back to One PP. Now be so kind as to help me out of my clothes. We have other things to accomplish."

"You really love the smell of salt air, don't you, Bobbie? You're never out of great ideas," I said as I removed her blouse. We went to the hot tub in our master bathroom, not the one by the pool. We didn't want to put on a show for Jane and Tilly.

CHAPTER **31**

Bobbie

Bob and I were amazed what our research dug up about elderly people being conned out of their money. We've all heard sporadic reports about these things, but neither of us knew how extensive the problem is. And it *is* extensive, quite extensive. I think we've put together a compelling case for Ralph. Hopefully he'll turn us loose on this. At least we had four wonderful days—and nights, at our place in East Hampton.

We walked into Ralph's office for our scheduled meeting. I was nervous that Ralph would find our plan to investigate Internet con jobs to be beneath the BBs. But shit, Bob and I have a love for seniors because we both had wonderful grandparents. Problem is, these cases usually fall below everybody's radar because they happen one at a time. There is usually no organized group to fight back.

I spent a lot of time with my grandparents because my folks were frequently too busy. They would often take me to that great amusement park in New Jersey, Six Flags. I was about 10 years old at the time, and that would have made them in their late 50s. I think they liked the rides as much as I did. When they were in their late 60s, I remember them being ripped off by a con man. It wasn't an Internet scam but a door to door home improvement fraud. Just as Evelyn Reynolds said about her mom, my grandparents were not stupid, but just very trusting. Too trusting. They lost $15,000 in that case, more than they could afford, especially because they got nothing to show for it.

Bob told me of a similar incident with his grandparents, a door to door home improvement conman. His grandparents lost over $7,000. It isn't like some group of people are being ripped off at the same time, a group that could appoint a leader and maybe hire a lawyer. These things happen one person or one couple at a time. Bob and I want to stop this shit, and who better than us.

When we walked into Ralph's office he was sitting behind his desk. As he always does, he stood to greet us. We told him about our conversation with Evelyn Reynolds, who Ralph knows as a frequent diner at her restaurant in East Hampton. We then told him about our experience with our own grandparents. What I think nailed it for him were the newspaper and magazine articles that our research dug up. At least journalists don't ignore this stuff.

Ralph then told us about his own parents' problems with Internet fraud. Just like Evelyn Reynolds, Ralph's mother fell for a call from a seemingly reputable company, warning her about a virus that had supposedly infected her computer. The guy then held her up for ransom. You would think the New York City police commissioner could have found the bastard, but these creeps are as skilled at hiding themselves as they are at stealing from people. Seeing no way out of the problem, Ralph's mom paid a $5,000 ransom and got her files back. From the look on Ralph's face as he told us that story, I could see that he was as pissed off as we were.

Ralph stood and went over to the table with the water pitcher, as he often does when pondering something.

"I agree with you guys. These poor people are being picked off one by one, and few of them can afford to hire a lawyer, not that a lawyer could do much against a skilled conman anyway. These are crimes that are being committed, and I thank you guys for focusing me on this. Hundreds of these rip offs happen every day, but only to one person at a time, and that's why it falls under our radar. I can't assign this to you as a full-time case, but I want you to do what you can to stop these crimes and lock up a few of the bastards. If the NYPD can't stop this shit with the BBs leading the charge, nobody can."

———————

The next day, Bob and I met with a woman named Marilyn Andrews, president of an organization known as the Senior Council. My research told me that the Senior Council is a nonprofit organization dedicated to helping elderly people avoid fraud. They handle everything from home improvement rip-offs to Internet scams. My research also told me that the Senior Council is a solid, reputable outfit.

"I'm amazed that two NYPD detectives are sitting here in front of me. It's been my experience that the police department scarcely cares about elderly people being defrauded. People have come to rely on us to act as their advocates, but I'm not sure what the hell I'm advocating. Yes, we do a good job educating seniors on how to avoid problems with fraud, but when it comes to pushing their cases in front of the police, we get stonewalled. Sure, they take down the information, but it never goes much further than that."

"There's a reason for that," I said. "Normal police procedures look at any fraud reports as one case at a time. Bob and I look at things differently, quite differently. We're looking at these cases as *one big case,* and that puts everything in a different perspective. And it gives the NYPD a reason to put some big budget resources behind it, especially Internet fraud, which is our main concentration. Let me tell you about a company called Small Apples."

"I never heard of it."

"That's because the organization really doesn't have a name, so we call it Small Apples. I'm sure you've heard about countless cases of a company, often masquerading as Apple or Microsoft, calling people to warn them that their computer has been infected with a virus. They then convince the victim to allow access to their computer. Once they're inside, all financial hell can break loose, and it usually does, everything from a simple ransom to raiding bank accounts."

"Is it really one company or group?" Marylin asked.

"We've narrowed it down to no fewer than 10 groups that are pulling off this crap. Bob and I are treating this group as a bunch of serial killers, and nobody knows more about fighting serial killers than Bob and I."

"Hey, wait a minute, I've heard and read about you two. You're the BBs, New York's famous detective team. Wow, when the NYPD puts its best detectives on the case, it tells me the department is finally taking this seriously. You two have locked up more serial killers than anybody, and I love the idea that you're looking at these bastards as serial killers, which they are—they kill elderly people's finances. Please think of me as your assistant. I'll do whatever I can to help you. I think it's brilliant that you're looking at all these matters as one big case."

"Do you have anything in your files that we can start working on?" Bob said.

Marilyn walked over to a file drawer and opened it.

"This entire drawer consists of Internet scam cases. We make duplicate copies of everything, so you're welcome to take these files with you."

"A major part of this, if not *the* major part," Bob said, "is prevention. Once somebody falls for the scam it's almost too late. I don't know about your budget, but I recommend making regular TV ads warning people about these frauds. I'm sure most networks will give you a break with public service announcements. You should say that you're working with the NYPD on this matter and that will help you get cooperation. Please pass by us the words of the announcements before you air them."

"Marilyn, here's a promise. Bob and I are going to put an end to this shit."

CHAPTER 32

Hello ladies and gentlemen. My name is Marilyn Andrews, president of the Senior Council, a not-for-profit organization with one goal—to protect senior citizens from fraud. If you're listening to me, please note my words carefully. Our city, not to mention our country, has seen a rapid increase in Internet fraud. It usually starts with a call, supposedly from a big well-known company like Microsoft or Apple. The person on the line tells you that your computer has been infected with a virus, and to solve the problem, you need to give him access to your computer. *Do not,* under any circumstances allow him access. We have seen everything from a ransom demand to out and out raids on bank accounts. Senior Council is working closely with the New York Police Department to try to bring an end to this criminal activity. If you receive such a call, ask the person to hold while you use your cellphone to call the number you see at the bottom of this screen. It's the special cyber-crime unit at the NYPD, and two of the department's best detectives are working with it. Give the officer the phone number of the person who called you on the other phone, and he will take it from there. Then hang up immediately. Together we will put an end to this horrible fraud. Thank you for listening."

CHAPTER 33

Bob

Bobbie and I felt that we had a good meeting with Marilyn Andrews, the head of that Senior Council outfit. When we spoke with her, we had the definite feeling that we were talking to a dedicated person, enthusiastic and dedicated.

"Those public service announcements that the Senior Council has been running are good, but not good enough," I said. "They're running 15 announcements a day across all the major networks. Putting our phone number on the screen is also a good idea, but we've got a problem. Wanna guess what it is?"

"Yeah, Bob, we've got a problem. Technology. The good part of phone technology means that we can trace a call immediately and not have to wait for 60 seconds as they do on TV cop shows. We've all heard the familiar dialog: 'Keep him on the line for 60 seconds, officer, while I put in a trace.' No longer happens that way. But the really *bad* news is a 'drop phone' also known as a 'burner phone,' devices that can't be traced. You can buy one of those goddam things at your nearest Walmart. The scammers may be slimy, but we can't assume they're stupid. Technology enables the bastards to hide in the weeds."

"At least those announcements will get through to some people who will simply hang up on the scammer," I said. "We may need to settle for cutting down on the odds."

"But we don't operate that way, do we honey?"

"No, we don't. Any suggestions?"

"I think we should turn loose our brilliant assistant, Joyce. She can regularly scan the Internet to see if she can come up with a name."

We called Joyce into our office and told her about our plans for finding Internet con artists.

"Don't worry, BBs. I'll nail those fucks."

Joyce, our pretty young assistant, has recently adopted the mouth of a hardened cop.

A week went by, then two. We had gotten no fewer than 20 calls from people who had a scammer on the phone. But just as we suspected, the thieves regularly use burner phones, so their calls could not be traced. Those devices may help with privacy, but they sure as hell make law enforcement a lot more challenging. Joyce has been drowning herself in Internet sites trying to find the name of a scammer.

The intercom sounded. It was Joyce.

"All of a sudden I've gotten some results. I just hope they're good ones. The names I've gotten came mainly from chat rooms and blogs. Here is one that turns up constantly—The Virus Killer. Despite the name, they don't kill viruses, they spread them. A lot of people are screaming about this organization but didn't call the police. What surprises me is how clumsy this outfit is. They may be sophisticated with technology, but they don't know how to cover their tracks. They have a website: viruskiller.com, and they didn't even hide their IP address. I asked Commissioner Ralph to get me a subpoena to get the physical address from Network Solutions, the web hosting site. It's right nearby in Jamaica, Queens. 2223 Sutphin Boulevard. The site administrator is a man named Aditya Hiral."

"Joyce, honey," Bobbie said, "have I mentioned recently that you're the best?"

"How about we pay that guy Hiral a visit, Bobbie?" I said. "Wanna come along, Joyce?"

I figured that our diligent assistant should get some onsite detective experience rather than spending all her time in front of a computer screen. Joyce clapped her hands, her face breaking out into a wide smile.

We met our driver in the parking lot and set off for the short trip to Jamaica. I first went to Ralph's office to get cleared for a search warrant. We could interrogate the guy without one, but I wanted to search his apartment in case we came up with something interesting.

After two rings a man came to the door.

"Are you Mr. Aditya Hiral?" I asked.

"Yes, what is this about?" he asked, with an unmistakable look of fear on his face.

"My name is Detective Bob Lawton. This is my partner, Detective Bobbie Nelson, and this is our assistant Joyce Randolph. We'd like to ask you a few questions."

"I have nothing to say to you."

"Well, maybe this will encourage you." I showed him the warrant.

We agreed that Bobbie would begin the questions, as her pretty face has a way of relaxing an interrogee. Of course, he didn't know it, but Bobbie is a killer of an interrogator.

"Mr. Hiral, are you familiar with a website called viruskiller. com?"

"I don't know what you're talking about." The guy may be a liar, but he's a very bad one, as his facial expression showed.

"The document that Detective Lawton showed you is a search warrant. While we talk, our assistant Detective Randolph will have a look around." Joyce smiled broadly after Bobbie referred to her as "Detective" Randolph. Joyce put on her latex gloves and began to snoop. She walked into a den and spent a few minutes looking at papers on the table next to a cellphone. She could tell from an insignia that it was a burner phone, one that couldn't be traced.

She walked back into the living room and handed me few sheets of paper stapled together.

"This looks like a phone script, Bob," Joyce said. "Maybe our friend here is a playwright."

I read aloud from the script.

"Hello, my name is (*made-up name*) and I'm with Microsoft. I regret to inform you that your computer has been hacked and you now have a dangerous virus on your system. I need to access your computer immediately to erase the threat. Any delay could result in all of your files being deleted."

The script went on to list various responses depending on what the person who answered the phone said.

Hiral sat there wearing a poker face.

I reached into my jacket pocket and retrieved handcuffs.

"Mr. Hiral, you're under arrest on suspicion of wire fraud and other crimes which will be disclosed to you at arraignment. You have the right to remain silent. Anything you say can and will be used against you in a court of law. You have the right to an attorney. If you cannot afford an attorney, one will be provided to you. Kindly put your hands behind your back."

I called our driver to help us move computer equipment and documents from the apartment.

I cuffed him and we escorted him to our car. Joyce looked excited as hell. She had never been in on an arrest before.

CHAPTER 34

Bobbie

On our way back to One PP I drafted a commendation that I'm going to hand to Commissioner Ralph about Joyce Randolph. That lady has a talent for nailing it. I'm going to recommend a raise and a promotion. Bob told me to make it above both our signatures.

When we arrived at the interrogation room at One PP, Mr. Hiral's court-appointed attorney, Hugo Quintal, was waiting for us. Bob and I know Quintal well from previous encounters. He's a good man and a good lawyer. I turned on the voice recorder and the surveillance video camera. Joyce was in the next room going through Hiral's computer that we seized with the search warrant.

"Mr. Hiral, are you familiar with this document?" I said, handing him the phone script.

"Objection, there is no foundation for this line of questioning," his attorney said.

"Let the record show that we obtained this document in your client's apartment next to a cellphone—known as a drop phone or burner phone, one that can't be traced. Our search was conducted pursuant to a warrant, a copy of which I'm handing to you now." I held up the warrant to the videocam.

"So, I repeat my question, sir, are you familiar with this document which is obviously a telephone script."

"Objection, how do you know it's a phone script?"

I handed him a copy of the script.

"Kindly read the document I just handed to you, counselor. Do you not agree that it is a script, or do I need to get an order from a judge to advise you of what is obvious?"

"Go ahead," Quintal said. I felt bad for him because there was little he could object to. When you're a court-appointed lawyer, you don't get to pick your clients, and sometimes you wind up with a piece of shit. "But I advise you, Mr. Hiral, you have the right to remain silent," he said.

But Hiral seemed to want to talk, which was good, because it helped to speed things along and not depend on a court hearing.

"So, I repeat my question, sir. Are you familiar with this document we found in your apartment?"

"I'm a computer consultant. I help people whose computers have been infected with a virus," Hiral said.

"And how do you know when someone's computer has become infected?"

"Objection, you're asking a question about something not in evidence."

"Pardon me, counselor, but your client just put it in evidence by saying that he helps people whose computers have been infected. How he knows about the infection is an obvious follow-up question."

Bob and I continued interrogating Hiral for about an hour, after which I called for an officer to escort Hiral to the lockup. As attorney Quintal was about to leave, I asked him if we could have a word with him.

"Hugo, (when not in the presence of a client, we call him by his first name) Bob and I are detectives, not prosecutors, but I'm letting you know right now what we're after, and we're sure the DA will agree. We want names, names of people and other Internet scamming organizations. I'm sure the DA will be open to a plea bargain with your charming client. Bob and I will personally talk to the DA about it. I normally wouldn't bring this up early in an investigation, but we want to move this case along quickly. Have a good day, Hugo. I hope your next court-appointed client isn't an asshole."

"Have I mentioned recently that you two are a pain in the ass?"

"Bob and I are proud to be pains in the ass."

CHAPTER 35

Bob

Bobbie and I obtained another warrant to search for Mr. Hiral's financial records. We were surprised, if not shocked, to see that this creep is well paid for his scamming. His net worth is over $4 million. When we get the names of his victims, at least they will have a shot at civil lawsuits, maybe a class action suit, to get some of their money back.

We consulted with the DA about a possible plea bargain in return for more names. Commissioner Ralph had already spoken to him about it. The criminal justice system could not exist without plea bargaining. The same goes with settlements in civil cases. If every case had to go to trial, the system would collapse like a mountain of bricks.

The next day, with an assistant district attorney present, we again interviewed Aditya Hiral. Hugo Quintal, the overworked and beleaguered lawyer, was there. Hiral was facing a possible 25-year sentence for his various scamming crimes. Dwight Munson, the assistant district attorney, on orders from the DA himself, offered Hiral five years off for every name he gave us, after first determining how many names he had. Hugo Quintal advised him to accept the deal, and he gave us three names.

None of the three names we got from Hiral were in New York, so commissioner Ralph once again called FBI Director Watson to deputize us as FBI agents.

On Bobbie's recommendation, seconded by mine, Ralph gave Joyce Randolph a promotion to full detective, Third Grade. After Ralph made the announcement, Bobbie and I took Joyce to lunch to congratulate her and to tell her how much we'd miss working with her.

"Are you guys shitting me? Working with the BBs is the best part of being with the NYPD. I spoke to Commissioner Ralph about this and he agreed to assign me to work with you two. I can cover for you when you go to your beautiful house in East Hampton. Hint, hint."

I cracked up and told her we were delighted to still work with her. I reached into my pocket and handed her a set of keys to our place in East Hampton.

"You and your husband can enjoy some salt air on Bobbie and me." She stood and walked around the table and hugged us both.

CHAPTER 36

Bob

Jane showed up promptly at 8 a.m. and immediately gave Tilly a hug. I think Jane is beginning to look at Tilly as her little sister.

That afternoon, Bobbie and I flew to Kansas City, where we would interrogate a man named Aarav Basak. We had obtained search warrants from the FBI. Our car drove us to the address we got from a subpoena on GoDaddy, the Internet service provider for a website called nomorevirus.com. Again, we were surprised that the man did not attempt to hide the IP address, enabling GoDaddy to surrender the physical address.

We pulled up in front of a nondescript suburban home. After we rang the bell three times, a man came to the door. He was short and somewhat skinny. He wore a turban and thick glasses. We wore our FBI badges. I introduced us and said we'd like to ask him a few questions. He let us in without an argument, which surprised me. I showed him our search warrant, and he led us into a small living room, where, I noticed, a computer workstation was against a wall. Bobbie said that she was going to look around, pursuant to the search warrant. She walked into an adjacent room where another workstation was located.

Then she walked back into the room and handed me a sheaf of papers.

"Looks like we have another playwright, Bob."

She walked back to the other room to continue searching.

I read the document, which, just as with our other suspect, was a script of questions to ask in a phone conversation, beginning with the familiar, "I am a representative of Microsoft, and I regret to inform you that your computer has been infected by an Internet virus…"

Bobbie continued to search the adjacent room as I read the script. When I looked up from what I was reading, I saw a Colt 45 pointed at my chest. I realized that if I tried to unholster my gun, I'd be killed. TV shows would make you think that detectives are gunslingers. Far from the truth. We are seldom involved in gunplay. I was scared shitless.

Blam, Blam, rang out two shots from the doorway to the next room. Basak slumped to the floor, dead. Bobbie holstered her Glock.

I stood and we hugged. What we thought would be a routine interrogation almost got me killed. Have I mentioned that I have the world's best partner?

Bobbie was crying. "This is the second time I almost lost you Bob," she said as she buried her face in my chest, her arms wrapped around me, squeezing.

"Yeah, and the second time you saved my life. I love you, Bobbie."

According to protocol, I called the Kansas City Police Chief to report what happened. Within four minutes we heard the siren as a patrol car pulled up in front of the house. A detective walked in along with a uniformed cop. The detective took our statement as he was required to. We called Commissioner Ralph's office to let him know we'd be in Kansas City for longer than we expected. Then we called Jane to let her know we would be gone for a few days. I suggested she invite her fiancé to join her while we were gone. Bobbie and I knew we may find some names on Basak's computer, and we may need to interrogate more people. But I wouldn't make the mistake I'd just made, and we planned to handcuff any future suspect for weapons. Interrogating a fraud suspect isn't supposed to be dangerous.

When we got to the Kansas City Police headquarters, we were greeted by Phil Toliver, the Kansas City Police Chief. We told him all about our investigation, and he looked happy to hear it.

"We've got a lot of elderly people here in Kansas City. I'm happy to see that the NYPD and the FBI is watching out for their asses," Chief Toliver said.

Bobbie and I spent the rest of the day at the Kansas City Police headquarters going over Basak's computer files. He regularly communicated with a guy named Bob Spencer, also from Kansas City. As we reviewed message after message, it became obvious that they were comparing notes on their scamming activities. One message jumped out at us. It was from Spencer to Basak.

"Nailed a good one today," Spencer wrote, "a $75,000 bank account. Took me all of 15 minutes. I used some of those new script lines you sent me. Worked like a charm. Later, buddy."

Bobbie looked at me. "Can you believe how stupid these guys are to write this stuff? They may be good scam artists, but they sure as hell don't know how to keep under cover."

Our research showed that these cyber warriors regularly hold up big companies with ransom demands, but never *too* big a demand.

They want to put corporate executives in a position to think it's easier to pay the ransom demand than it is to lose their files. The same goes for the poor elderly folks they victimize. The typical corporate ransom demand is under $50,000 and the typical senior citizen demand is under $5,000. The crooks want to make it easy to say yes to a ransom demand.

We spent two hours going over Basak's files. We found three more names who we think are scammers based on the wording of their messages. We got their addresses from Basak's contact list. Their names are Michael Bollinger, from Fairfield, Connecticut, Thomas Lang, from Parsippany, New Jersey, and Walter Denton, from Manhattan. We were happy to see that the suspects are nearby to our place in New York, because we both want to spend some quality time with Tilly.

Bobbie has become quite convincing in her search warrant applications and managed to persuade the judge to give us search warrants for the three new names. Bobbie made sure to include the fact that I was almost killed in one of our interrogations. It put the judge on notice that we're dealing with some bad people.

CHAPTER 37

Bobbie

Bob and I had a busy week interrogating our next three cyber-crime suspects, Michael Bollinger, Thomas Lang, and Walter Denton. Bob and I took turns interrogating the men and executing the search warrants. This time we made sure to place the suspect in handcuffs while we interrogated them. We also brought two uniformed cops with us. No way in hell do I want to see Bob shot. Or me, for that matter. Based on the evidence disclosed by our interrogations, we placed each of the three under arrest. Maybe they can scam their cellmates.

We felt good that we had broken the fraud rings that preyed on elderly people. But our work soon got the attention of both Sarah Watson and Rick Bellamy. Our mission went beyond protecting senior citizens and now includes cybercrime in general. The computer brains behind the FBI Cyber-Crime Unit worked on the complex details, even though I'm pretty good at technical stuff. It would become our job to interrogate suspects that the Cyber Crime Unit dug up. Not a full-time assignment, but an interesting and rewarding one. I love to lock up creeps.

Tomorrow is Saturday and we want to spend the weekend with Tilly. We will head for East Hampton. We invited our babysitter Jane Romelli and told her to bring along Steve Rankin, her fiancé. Jane was becoming more of a governess than a babysitter and that was fine with her. Watching over Tilly doesn't take up all her hours, and she had plenty of time to work on her latest novel. We volunteered to beta read the latest draft, a crime thriller entitled *A Gun Too Far*. A lot of the police background for the book came from our bestseller, *Detectiving*, which I was happy to see. A big part of the idea behind *Detectiving*, as our publisher reminds us, is to provide accurate background for crime novelists. I found it touching, as did Bob, that the two major protagonists in the book, a couple of married detectives, were patterned after us.

We pulled up to our East Hampton house at 11:45 on Saturday morning. Jane, who loves to cook, God bless her, prepared lunch, including scrambled eggs and grits for Tilly. After we ate, Bob and I took little Tilly for a walk in her stroller. We headed for the village shops. Jane opened her laptop and dove into the latest draft of her novel. Steve Rankin, Jane's fiancé, worked out in our gym. I think they like it here. We spent the rest of the day pushing Tilly around in her stroller as we shopped the antique stores of East Hampton. As we passed a toy store, Bob made right turn and entered. Bob can't help himself when it comes to buying toys for our little girl.

We got back to our Manhattan apartment on Tuesday. During our ride, Bob asked me why I was so quiet all day long. He was right, I was quiet. I was quiet because something was bothering the hell out of me. He'd soon find out.

CHAPTER 38

Bobbie

"Hey, Bob, who is Marcie?"

"I don't know."

"You don't know? Last night after we made love you said, 'I love you Marcie.' I often hear you say her name out loud in your sleep. So, I repeat my question: Who is Marcie?"

"I don't know," Bob said.

He doesn't know? I've been a detective long enough to know when I hear bullshit, and that's what Bob just gave me—bullshit. He keeps saying the word Marcie in his sleep and now he tells me he doesn't know anybody by that name. Last night, he even said her name while he was awake. He blamed it on having one too many martinis. But why would a martini make you say the name Marcie? I think Bob and I have a strong marriage, but that name Marcie is driving me nuts. Bob is intoxicatingly handsome, and maybe I'm naïve, just imagining that he must keep fending off the constant flirtations he gets from women. I've seen women almost throw themselves at Bob. Am I stupid enough to think that he doesn't notice, and that he is so emotionless not to enjoy it? I have a sick feeling in my stomach. Can Bob, *my* Bob, have a mistress? A mistress named Marcie?

I remember vividly that dream I kept having when I was in the hospital, the one where he was screwing that beautiful brunette on a desk. Was it just a delusion, just a bad dream, or was it a recollection of something I actually saw? Maybe it really happened—and maybe her name was Marcie.

But he keeps denying that he knows somebody named Marcie. I'm having a feeling that I hate, a feeling that's killing me, a feeling that's totally unfamiliar about something I could never imagine.

Bob is lying to me.

CHAPTER 39

Bob

I never keep anything from Bobbie. That's the way it is with us, complete honesty. But one thing I *have* kept from her is Marcie. I think it's because of the pain I feel when I think of Marcie, a pain that won't let me talk about her, a pain I don't want to share, a pain I just want to go away. But I realized that the time had come. I need to be completely open with Bobbie about Marcie. No way in hell would I let my Bobbie think that something is going on with me and another woman. I know that she thinks I'm lying to her, the last thing I'd ever want to do. But I *am* lying, I have been lying—about Marcie.

Bobbie walked into the den after putting Tilly to bed.

"Bobbie, can we talk?"

"Hasn't seemed like you wanted to talk recently," Bobbie said, her face looking like she just stepped in dog shit. "If you don't want to tell me about a woman named Marcie, I don't want to talk. Tell me about her or we'll never talk again. Who the hell is she?"

Oh my God, that hurt. Never talk again? Okay, it's time to be open and honest with Bobbie. I took a deep breath.

"Second Lieutenant Marcie Sullivan was my administrative officer when I commanded that rifle company in Iraq. She was amazingly efficient at her job, and I relied on her to keep the company organized and running smoothly, while I concentrated on killing the enemy. As the months went by, I found myself meeting with her often, usually making up excuses to tell myself why I wanted to meet with her. But most of the time, it was for no reason other than I enjoyed being with her. She seemed to enjoy being with me. I found myself quite attracted to her, and I think she felt the same way about me."

"Tell me about her looks?" Bobbie asked, her face looking like she wanted to throw up.

"She was beautiful, even in Marine combat fatigues. Until I met you, Marcie Sullivan was the best-looking woman I'd ever seen. But I was strict as hell in my role as company commander, and I would never let my feelings show for a junior officer. Marcie, a disciplined officer herself, was just as much a stickler as me when it came to military protocol. But we'd meet often because our jobs required it, and because I just enjoyed meeting with her. And I think she enjoyed meeting with me. I began to notice that our eyes would often engage one another, and then the glances began to linger."

The look on Bobbie's face felt like a punch to my stomach. But I continued on with the story of Marcie Sullivan.

"We were both scheduled to muster out of the Corps on the same day. She had accepted a job as an instructor at American University in Washington, and I had some job interviews lined up in Washington. One day, about a month before we were scheduled to muster out, I threw my military discipline to the wind, and asked her if we could get together for dinner when we got back to the States. She readily agreed. So, we would soon go out on a date. We both realized that we were becoming attracted to each other, but somehow managed to keep our military discipline together."

"Did you love her, Bob?"

I swallowed hard.

"Yes, I did."

"Where is she now?"

"Exactly one week before we were scheduled to leave, our company was attacked by the enemy with RPGs and bullets. I managed to keep it together and prevented our company from being overrun."

"Was that the action for which you won the Bronze Star for heroism?"

"Yes, it was. So, my company wasn't overrun but a few of my people were killed—including Lieutenant Marcie Sullivan. We never did have our date in Washington. The last time I saw her, she was in a body bag. Half her head had been blown away."

CHAPTER 40

Bobbie

When Bob told me that the last time he saw Marcie Sullivan she was in a body bag, I thought I'd never stop crying. I wrapped my arms around Bob, trying desperately to make his pain go away. But my tears were mixed with other emotions.

I Googled the words "Marcie Sullivan Marine," and got a bunch of hits, including photos. My God, what a beautiful young woman. It wasn't difficult to see why Bob fell for her. When Bob poured his heart out to me about Marcie, there was one part of the story that actually made me happy—the part where she was killed in a rocket attack. I felt like an absolute total shit. I was happy that she was dead? If she wasn't, Bob would not be mine, he would be hers. But Bob *is* mine, not hers—because the poor woman was killed. Sometimes your mind wanders to bad places, really bad places, disgustingly bad places. What kind of heartless bitch am I? I actually felt a weird kind of joy at the death of that beautiful young lieutenant. I downloaded the best picture of her and printed it out. Tilly was napping and Bob was in the living room reading. I walked up to him and showed him the photo of Marcie.

"Bob, I want you to share Marcie with me. I want her to be part of our history, part of our lives, part of *my* life. I want to frame this photo and put it on our mantel."

Bob stood and wrapped his arms around me.

"It's not like I gave up on her or did anything to stop our budding relationship. She was just killed."

"Bob, you were decorated for heroism because of the lives you saved that day. But, as fate would have it, you didn't save the most important person."

"Yeah, it was a pretty rough period in my life."

"Did you ever get to share with each other the fact that you were in love?"

"Yes. The night before she was killed, we said that we loved each other."

Bob hugged me again. Now, *he* was crying. My God, I love this man. Suddenly I felt a different emotion about Marcie Sullivan. I felt sorry for her, sorry for the loss of her young life. She loved Bob, and who could blame her. Now she's gone, but, understandably, Bob still has feelings for her. Yes, understandably. And so do I. I resolved to keep Marcie Sullivan in my mind as my guardian angel, an angel who sent Bob to me. Somehow thinking about Marcie Sullivan that way makes me feel less guilty about having doubted Bob's loyalty to me. I told Bob about my guardian angel thoughts and we both broke down again.

Tilly woke up and started to fuss and we both went to her room. Bob picked her up and handed her to me, kissing me first.

"We have a lot of love in our lives, don't we Bob?"

"We sure do, honey, we sure do," he said, wrapping his big arms around me and Tilly.

CHAPTER 41

Bob

The word relief doesn't quite capture how I felt after I finally got my shit together and told Bobbie about Marcie Sullivan, a beautiful young woman who I once loved, and who once loved me. A beautiful young woman who was killed. Bobbie's reaction to the story made me realize what an asshole I had been in keeping it from her. Bobbie's reaction was also typical of her— full of love and compassion. She held me constantly after I told her about Marcie, as if she was trying to squeeze the sadness out of me. And then she said she'll always think of Marcie Sullivan as her guardian angel, and that she brought Bobbie and me together. I always think of myself as a tough cop, not one to cry easily. But when Bobbie said that Marcie is her guardian angel, I broke down in tears, big tears, sobbing tears.

Bobbie's not part of my life—she *is* my life.

––––––––––

The next morning, Bobbie went back to our apartment to check up on Tilly, who was running a slight temperature. My friend, Detective Mike Simpson walked into my office. He looked upset about something.

"What's up Mike, why the puss?"

"I cannot fucking believe this, Bob. I just came back from the animal shelter. My dog ran away and I went there to retrieve him. Thank God he was okay."

"So, you should be happy you found him, no?"

"Yes, but get this, something I didn't know about animal shelters. There was this cute little French Bulldog puppy in a cage. On the cage was a sign with the number 17. I asked the attendant what the number was all about and he said that is the order in which the little puppy would be euthanized. Its master had been killed in a car accident and nobody had claimed the dog. That put him in line to be killed."

"Where is the animal shelter?" I asked.

He gave me the address. Three blocks from One PP.

Sometimes I act on instinct, something all detectives to do on occasion. For some reason, I just had to go to the shelter to see that dog. I *had* to go; it wasn't an option. Mike had described it as quite small, with a white coat.

Twenty minutes later I walked into the shelter. Against the wall was a cage that contained the dog Mike had told me about. At the back of the cage sat a little French Bulldog that can only be described with one word—adorable. The sign on front of the cage bore the number 11. Mike had told me that he saw the number 17 on the cage. Shit, I thought, this little puppy is marching toward its death. I could swear that he looked at me with a face that said, "Please take me home with you." I decided to let a rational thought enter my mind, although I was feeling anything but rational. I know Bobbie likes dogs, and we've discussed getting one, but I needed to check with our irreplaceable babysitter, Jane Romelli. What if she doesn't get along with dogs? I dialed her cellphone. When she answered, I asked the big question: "Jane, do you like dogs?"

"I don't like dogs, I *love* dogs."

"Great, I'm going to be there shortly with a little surprise. Not a word to Bobbie about this call, okay?"

"Oh my God," Jane said. "I can't wait."

I filled out the paperwork, scooped up the tiny puppy, and walked to our apartment.

I walked in with the puppy nestled under my jacket. Jane looked at me with eyes as big as softballs. I opened my jacket to give Jane a peek. "Bobbie's in Tilly's room," she said with a big smile on her face as she reached over to give the puppy a scratch under his chin. She followed me in. No way did Jane want to miss the show.

"Look what just fell from heaven into my arms," I said to Bobbie, reaching into my jacket and holding out the puppy to her.

"Oh my God, he's adorable!" Bobbie said, as the puppy smothered her face with licking kisses. "Please tell me you adopted him?"

"How could I *not* adopt him? He was on a list to be euthanized."

Bobbie held my face in her free hand and kissed me, her other hand busy fondling the puppy. "Have I mentioned recently how much I love you, Bob? What should we call him?"

"I'm thinking Sherlock. Didn't the *Chicago Tribune* once call Bobbie Nelson a real-life Sherlock Holmes? Now we can match the name to a face."

Tilly was standing, holding onto the rail of her crib, with the biggest smile I'd ever seen on her. Bobbie held out little Sherlock to Tilly and the puppy immediately washed her face in kisses.

"Lucky," Tilly screamed.

Bobbie looked at me, then at Jane. "Looks like the puppy's name is Lucky, not Sherlock."

Bobbie handed Lucky to Jane, who immediately held him out to Tilly.

"Where will we walk him?" Bobbie asked, always the careful planner.

"Perfect solution," Jane said. "Tilly and I can walk him on the grassy area of your rooftop garden when you guys are at the office. I can flick his business into the bushes with a shovel, although a teaspoon will probably do the trick."

"Today is Thursday," I said. "Bobbie and I are planning on going to our house in East Hampton. Would you and Steve like to join us?"

"Oh, wow, yes! Steve and I love your house. I'll go with you guys and Steve will drive out on Saturday morning."

So, our growing family will be heading east.

CHAPTER 42

Bobbie

On Friday morning we headed east for a few days of fun. Jane sat in the back with Lucky on her lap. Tilly sat next to Jane with her head on her shoulder, stroking Lucky all the while.

As Bob pulled into the driveway, Maggie, our neighbor's Golden Retriever, came bounding over to greet us. I put Lucky on the ground, and Maggie looked like she just saw heaven. She dropped to the ground with that typical Golden pose, her front paws splayed out in front of her, looking at Lucky with a face that said, "Let's play." She slurped Lucky's face as if it were an ice cream cone. Lucky rolled over, loving it. Jane kneeled next to them, joined by Tilly.

When we walked into the house I was struck by that wonderful familiar feeling. This house gets bigger every time I look at it. Buying this place was one of the best moves Bob and I ever made. From the look on Tilly's face, it seems that Bob's rescue of that little puppy was a great move too. Bob has a wonderful habit of getting it right.

It's obvious that little Lucky loves Tilly. All Tilly needs to do is call the dog's name and it comes running. I can't get over how Tilly's vocabulary grows every day, and it's because of Jane who constantly works with her. Jane, the babysitter sent from heaven.

Jane reached into her briefcase and came out with two documents, one for me and one for Bob. It was the fifth draft of her crime novel, *A Gun Too Far*. Bob and I had volunteered to beta read the book for her, and we were happy that we would now have the opportunity to dig into it. She patterned the two main characters after guess who—Bob and me. As I sat on the terrace reading through the 249-page manuscript, I had an unsettled feeling in my stomach. Jane is a brilliant writer, and I'm afraid that we'll lose the best governess we could ever imagine. But Bob reminds me that Jane is more than a part-time employee. She's adopted us. She's become a part of our family. And her babysitting job enables her to write. She has an amazing attention span. I would often watch her, even while she played with Tilly, that she would pound out a few words between Tilly's need for attention. I wish I could write like that.

As I read through Jane's book, I thought I was reading a screenplay about Bob and me. The characters even had alliterative names, like Bob and Bobbie—Al and Ally. When the two detectives are partnered, they were both 35 years old. Sound familiar? Ally was even hired from another state, just like me. From her description of Bob's (Al's) physical appearance, it's obvious that she spends a lot of time looking at him, not that I blame her. She described my character as "strikingly beautiful," which I thought was a bit over the top, but I must admit I felt flattered. She even nailed the early days of our partnership, including the rough spots. Obviously, she listened carefully when Bob and I told her our story. Then she let her keen imagination take over. Her description of the first time Al and Ally made love was a bit X-rated. I didn't recall going into *that* much detail about Bob and me. But it clearly came from the creative mind of a talented novelist. Another key character was the police commissioner, Roy Lundquist. Like Ralph Norquist? Her description of the heavy cases that Al and Ally work on was spot-on perfect. Besides interviewing us to get her police stuff right, she clearly had done a lot of serious research. In her acknowledgements, she praised our book *Detectiving* for its detailed descriptions of the art of being a detective. She also acknowledged Bob and me for helping her when she interviewed us on technical matters.

When we finished marking up our manuscripts, Bob and I compared notes. It was a touchingly well-told story, with all sorts of fascinating plot twists and a drop-dead killer ending. I thought I was reading an author from *The New York Times* Best Seller list.

"When I read about Detective Ally, I thought I was reading about you, honey," Bob said. "Wow, she's sexy, just like another detective I know."

"And I don't need to tell you who Detective Al reminds me of, Mr. Handsome-Hunk," I said.

We gave our edited manuscripts to Jane. There was little editing by either of us. Besides being a tremendous writer, Jane is also a careful proofreader. I couldn't believe this was only draft number five.

Bob, Jane and I sat down on our terrace, taking in the breathtaking view of Georgica Pond and sipping coffee. Tilly sat on Jane's lap, playing with her necklace. Lucky was curled up by my feet, licking my ankles.

"Do you have the electronic version of the manuscript on your laptop, Jane?"

"Sure. I never go anywhere without it. Why do you ask?"

"Bob and I just got off the phone with a guy named Tom Cunningham. He's the editor-in-chief of Random House, the company that published our book, *Detectiving*. He wants to see your manuscript."

"Oh my God. Random House? But I think it needs to go through a few more drafts, Bobbie."

"Sure, everything always needs a few more drafts, but Bob and I think it's in excellent shape right now and we told Tom Cunningham so. He sounded really excited about your book, and he's not a guy to exaggerate. He wants to look at it as soon as possible. Why don't you email the manuscript to me and I'll email it to Tom with a cover letter from both Bob and me."

"How can I possibly thank you enough? I think you guys are my best friends." She started to cry, and Tilly wiped her tears away.

"Thank you for saying that, honey. Bob and I think of you as our sister, not just a friend. And Tilly loves you. Nothing would make her happier to see her buddy Jane become a big-time author."

"It's time for Tilly's nap," Jane said. "While she's asleep I'd like to jump into the pool if you don't mind."

"Of course, we don't mind."

"I need some serious exercise to keep my head from exploding. Oh my God—Random House!"

———

At 2:30, our erstwhile assistant, Joyce Randolph and her husband showed up.

"Hi, Detective Joyce. Glad you and Mike can join us," I said. Joyce beamed at the word "detective." I was happy as hell that Bob and I recommended her promotion, and so was Joyce. Mike Randolph is a slim, handsome guy, about six foot. He's a professor of management at Columbia University. He and Joyce got married last year, before we knew Joyce. I showed them to their room, and they freaked out over the view of Georgica Pond. Bob and I think of our assistant Joyce as a good friend, a very talented friend. I've never seen anyone better than her at wading through complicated data, and I'm pretty good at it myself.

They changed into their swimsuits and went to the pool, where Jane was working on her 50th lap. I walked down to introduce them to Jane, who was just climbing out of the pool.

"Why don't you and Bob get into your swimsuits," Jane said. "I'll be back down when Tilly wakes up from her nap."

Jane went to Tilly's room, wrapped in a bathrobe.

Bob went to the puppy's pen and picked up Lucky to introduce her to our friends. Then we went into the pool house to get into our bathing suits.

"Oh, my God," Joyce yelled when she saw Lucky. "Can I hold him?"

"Of course. He's a born snuggler," I said.

Maggie, the Golden Retriever from next door, came bounding up next to the pool and jumped in. Our neighbors Marge and Tim are embarrassed at Maggie's intrusiveness, but we keep reminding them that Maggie is always welcome at our house, especially because little Lucky now has friend to play with. Maggie paddled up to Joyce, who was holding the puppy. Lucky enjoyed a few huge face slurps from Maggie.

Bob and I dried off and went inside to change. Our master suite is so big and private, a convention could go on in the rest of the house and we'd never hear it.

"Hey, Bob, do you know what time it is?"

"It's four o'clock," He said.

"No, I didn't mean that. It's time to make love."

I peeled off my bikini and wrapped my arms around him. The feeling of his hard erection pressing against me told me that he was in the mood for love too. I pushed his swimsuit down to the floor and knelt before him, taking him into my mouth, looking up at his gorgeous face. I licked the tip, then went down the shaft.

"I hate to say stop what you're doing, but I want to be inside you." He lifted me onto the bed, spread my legs, and inserted himself into me, moving in and out, gently, slowly bringing me to a wonderful orgasm. I rolled over to catch my breath. I reached down and found that he was still obviously in the mood.

"My goodness," I said. "You're still hard."

"That's because I'm not done yet."

There's something about the salt air.

Forty-five minutes later Bob and I walked downstairs and out onto the patio to join the others for some afternoon drinks. We were both exhausted, wonderfully exhausted. No matter whatever else goes on in my life, making love with Bob is up there with the best.

From the smiles on everyone's faces I think they knew that Bob and I weren't napping.

Jane put some snacks on the patio table.

"I saw that guy walk by the house just before," Jane said. "He gives me the creeps, especially the way he looks at me and smiles. Maybe you detectives are rubbing off on me, but I have the feeling that he's stalking this house."

"I know who Jane is talking about, Bob," I said. "He gives me the creeps too. He sure walks by here a lot, always staring at the house, and often at Jane or me."

"I think I saw the same guy about an hour ago," Joyce said. "He looked at me and smiled. He made my skin crawl. Just like Jane said, I got the feeling he was stalking this house."

"Please point this guy out to me the next time you see him," Bob said. "See if you can get a photo of him when he's not looking your way."

My cellphone rang. It was Commissioner Ralph.

"I know you guys are taking a few days off, but can you be back here by Tuesday?"

"We were planning on that anyway, Ralph. Is there something big for us to take a look at?"

"Yeah, big. Really big, Bobbie."

"Can you hum the first few bars?"

"I'd rather it be a surprise, although not a happy one. See you Tuesday."

CHAPTER 43

Bob

We got back to our Manhattan apartment Monday evening at 6:30. We told Steve that he was more than welcome to stay overnight in Jane's room if he liked, to save him his trip to Westchester. It's a suite with an attached full bathroom. He graciously accepted our invitation. These two are definitely becoming part of our family.

We had breakfast with Jane, Steve, and Tilly. Lucky, the happy puppy, insisted on sitting on Jane's lap.

Bobbie and I were dying to learn about the new case Ralph has for us. When we walked into Ralph's office, he stood to greet us. But he wasn't smiling.

"A child kidnapping ring," he said. "These animals are kidnapping the children of wealthy people and holding them for huge ransoms." I could see why he wasn't smiling. Bobbie and I are wealthy—and we have a little girl.

"Are the ransoms being paid?" I asked,

"Yes. One couple of assholes decided to call the kidnappers bluff and wouldn't pay, assuming the guy would release their kid in spite of the ransom not being paid. The body of the ten-year old boy was found a week later. I want to turn loose my best detectives on this case, and obviously that means the BBs. Now I need to ask you a flat-out question. You two have quite a few bucks, God knows, and you recently adopted that beautiful little girl. Can you handle this assignment emotionally?"

"Yes," we both said. I didn't add that I might just shoot the fucks if we find them.

"Don't worry about us, Ralph. Bobbie and I know what we're doing."

"I doubt that anybody would be so stupid to mess with a couple of seasoned detectives, but I want to ask you a question. Is that charming babysitter of yours licensed to carry a firearm?"

Holy shit. Until Ralph just said that, I hadn't thought of it. Looks like Bobbie and I are going to want to beef up security.

"No, I don't believe Jane carries a gun," I said, swallowing hard.

"Any leads at all so far?" Bobbie asked.

"Not one," Ralph said. "I wish the government would outlaw those goddam burner phones that can't be traced. In each of the nine cases so far, the ransom demand was sent in a package with a recording of the instructions. Those were followed up with untraceable phone calls. Because the ransom demands and negotiations all were similar, we think there is only one ring involved. All the demands insisted that the ransom be paid in cash and shipped to a bank box in the Cayman Islands, each to a different location. Those banker whores wouldn't even dream about disclosing the name of a depositor. This is a tough one, BBs, but I know you'll get it done."

That afternoon Bobbie and I met with the head of Metro Security, a company we'd had positive dealings with in the past. Her name is Beverly Johnson, and she knows her stuff. She was a detective with the NYPD for many years, and now concentrates on hardening targets for companies and individuals. We introduced her to Jane Romelli and Tilly. Little Lucky took an immediate liking to Beverly and followed her around the apartment. Beverly toured every square inch of the apartment, making notes as she did, Lucky licking her ankles all the while.

"I recommend changing the locks on your doors every six months," Beverly said, "and putting in motion detectors that can be turned on and off with the click of a button. You may want to consider surveillance cameras in every room that you can view from your office at One PP. I also suggest that your babysitter wear an electronic device that can alert you in a moment. I hate to sound paranoid about this stuff, but it's my job. Later I'll email you a list of my recommendations—encrypted email, of course."

Beverly, as I knew from previous dealings with her, is quite a professional. We arranged for her to visit our house in East Hampton the following weekend. I couldn't help thinking about that mysterious guy in East Hampton who Jane, Joyce, and Bobbie think may be stalking our house. Jane managed to get of photo of the guy, thank goodness. The next time we're out East I think I'll introduce myself to him.

We would be home for the evening, so Jane took off at the same time as Beverly. After they left, Bobbie grabbed my hand.

"Are we being crazy, Bob?"

"No, we're not. We're being cautious. We're being responsible." I was looking at Tilly when I said that.

The next day we would see that we were not being overly cautious.

CHAPTER 44

Bobbie

The next day, Bob and I began working the kidnapping cases. We had a total of 10 cases to investigate, three of them active. By active, I mean that the kidnapped children are still missing. Because we assumed that the parents were under constant surveillance by the kidnappers, we arranged to interview them at the rectory office at St. Mark's Episcopal Church. Father Rick, our friend and pastor, graciously okayed the plan. No way could we risk having the parents to come to One PP, nor could we risk going to their house. One of the three parent couples in the active cases were Jewish, so we made a similar arrangement to interview them at our friend Rabbi Jacob's nearby synagogue. We didn't want to raise any question by risking them being seen entering an Episcopal church. When you're working an active case, you *never* want to raise questions. Detective work means careful work.

This afternoon we will interview Grace and Walter Baumgartner at St. Mark's. Their five-year old daughter, Tanya, went missing two days ago. They received the ransom demand and instructions last night, via a recording in a package delivered by UPS. The ransom demand was for $100,000. In all of the cases we've studied so far, the demand was never astronomical, and was always well within the means of the child victim's parents. The Baumgartners, owners of a software company, were quite wealthy, easily able to cover the $100,000 demand. This morning, following the instructions to the letter, they put the cash into a package and sent it to a bank in the Cayman Islands. They paid the exorbitant same-day delivery fee. They fidgeted, constantly looking at their cellphones, awaiting the instructions about where they could pick up their daughter.

The call finally came, the package having been apparently delivered. I had attached a recording device to each of their phones, but it did no good. The voice on the other end was heavily disguised. The voice said that little Tanya was inside St. Ann's Catholic Church in lower Manhattan. I suggested they take an Uber car to pick her up. They both looked like emotional wrecks and I was concerned about either one of them driving. No way could I assign a patrol car, even an unmarked one, because we had to assume the possibility that the pick-up would be under surveillance. Bob and I also thought it would be a bad idea for us to go with them. Our faces are well known, and if the Baumgartners were under surveillance, that could blow the rest of our investigation. They agreed they would bring Tanya to St. Mark's so we could question her.

Forty minutes later the Baumgartners walked in, along with Tanya, a cute little five-year old redhead. Tanya seemed happy and not the least bit upset. If an expression on a face can be described as relieved, that was the look on the Baumgartners. Grace never once let go of Tanya's hand.

"Can you tell us anything about the man or people you were with?" I said. I didn't say "who held you" or "who captured you," as I wanted Tanya to feel relaxed and free to talk.

"It was a man," Tanya said. "He was really nice, and gave me all kinds of good food, even chocolate chip cookies." No surprise so far. Kidnappers want money, not trouble. They're notorious for being polite with their captives, especially if they're children.

"Can you tell us what he looked like?" I said.

"He was a tall guy, kind of bald.

"Here's a picture of him."

"A picture!" all four of us loudly blurted. Poor Tanya looked like we scared the hell out of her.

"That's okay, honey," Grace said as she patted her hair. "You just kind of surprised us with the photo."

"He had a lot of pictures on his desk, and I figured he wouldn't mind if I took one. Am I in trouble for doing that?"

"No, honey," Bob said, "not at all."

God bless her, she just may have blown this case wide open.

Bob stared intently at the photo and then handed it to me. The photo was perfectly clear, with a head-on frontal view. We both agreed that the man looked familiar. Facial recognition software, here we come.

"Was there anybody else there besides this man?" Bob said.

"I heard a lady's voice in the next room, but I never saw her."

"Did the lady or this man speak with any kind of accent?" I asked.

"The lady didn't but the man sounded exactly like Uncle Peter."

I looked at her parents with a question mark on my face.

"My brother Peter speaks with a heavy German accent."

We then asked Tanya if she could describe her surroundings.

"It was an office," was all she said.

"Do you remember how you got there?" I asked, feeling like it was a dumb question. It was, but I had to ask it.

"No, the guy gave me these cool glasses that had cartoons playing on the inside of them. That's all I saw."

Just to nail down what we just heard, I picked up the photo and pointed toward it and said. "So, this man sounds just like your Uncle Peter?"

"Yes, *exactly* like Uncle Peter."

Walter reached over and handed Bob a business card. "Here's Peter's number. I'm sure you'll want to speak to him and maybe record his voice. I'll give him a heads up that you'll be calling."

"Thanks, Walter," Bob said, "you'd make a good detective. Hey, you folks look tired. I think we're done here for today. We'll be in touch if we make any progress on the case. But at least it had a happy ending. Thank God, Tanya is okay."

"From what I've heard about you BBs, I expect you'll soon be making a lot of progress," Grace said.

They left.

Bob and I hopped into our car and headed straight for One PP. So, we've got a clear photo and a description of a heavy German accent. I was feeling a lot better about this case than I did this morning.

CHAPTER 45

Bob

Bobbie and I sat in our office while the facial recognition people upstairs worked on the photo of our German-accented kidnapper. Our old friend, Detective-Psychiatrist Bennie Weinberg, always reminds us that all criminals eventually make a mistake. It always happens, Bennie insists. And it seems our kidnapper made a big one. He left photographs of himself within easy reach of his little kidnap victim.

While we waited on the photo recognition technicians, I called Peter Baumgartner, Walter's brother, the man who little Tanya said sounds just like her abductor. Peter is a patent lawyer with a firm in Manhattan.

"Baumgartner here," he said with Germanic efficiency. I explained the purpose of my call.

"Ya, Walter said you vould be calling. God bless you, Detective, for your vork on protecting our little Tanya."

"Well, it was your brother's money that did the work. Now it's up to my partner and me to try to put this creep behind bars, and maybe get some of Walter's money back."

"Walter told me that Tanya said her abductor had a charming German accent yoost like mine. I'm more than villing to having my voice recorded. How about I read a coople of paragraphs from today's newspaper?"

When Peter stopped reading, I thanked him profusely.

"Anything I can do to help you lock up that son of a bitch who stole our little Tanya, I'm only too happy to help."

Just as I got off the phone with Peter Baumgartner, Peggy Maxwell, the supervisor of the facial recognition department walked in.

"You BBs have a way of getting the job done, don't you?" Peggy said as she spread out some photos on our desk.

"Well, a five-year-old girl got this job done. All we did was deliver the goods to you folks. So, anything you can tell us about mysterious kidnapper?"

"Let me just let you two peruse these photos for a minute, then you tell me."

We looked at the photos of the man, including the one that little Tanya took from his office.

"Holy shit, Adolph Gunther!" we both said, with Bobbie contributing the holy shit.

"Yup, none other than Adolph Gunther," Peggy said. "One of the slimiest sons of bitches on the planet. He's got a friggin rap sheet the size of the Manhattan phone book. Everything from extortion, embezzling, to kidnapping—yes, kidnapping."

"Do you know if he speaks with a German accent?" Bobbie asked.

"Just check this out." She held up her iPad and played a clip. And there was that guy from the photos talking to someone off camera.

"Ja, zass is goot, frauline, zass is very goot."

"In the clip I just played he was reporting to a colleague on the result of a wire fraud scam they just handled. Obviously, he didn't know he was being videoed. Do you know where to find this guy?"

"No, the little girl he abducted had no idea where he took her, but from the timing of the events we believe it was somewhere in Manhattan. The girl said he sounded exactly like her Uncle Peter. Listen to this."

I played the recording that Peter Baumgartner made for us. Peggy looked amazed.

"So, looks like you've found your guy."

"Yeah," Bobbie said. "But where the hell *is* he?"

Bobbie grabbed for her phone.

"What are you doing, hon?"

"I'm calling in an APB. We'll find this bastard."

CHAPTER 46

Bob

When Jane walked into our apartment the next morning, she wore the biggest smile I had ever seen on her. Then she gave Bobbie and me bigger than her usual bear hugs. Then she scooped up Tilly, with Lucky licking her ankles.

"Something tells me you have something exciting to tell us," Bobbie said.

"Random House is going to publish my book, *A Gun Too Far*! I cannot friggin believe it. If it weren't for you two guys this never would have happened. You sure gave that guy Tom Cunningham a big introduction for me for me. Oh, my God, what would I do without you two?"

"So, tell us about the particulars," I said.

"He even offered me an advance—$50,000. I feel like I'm living a dream."

"Fifty thousand?" I said. "That's fabulous for a new star on the horizon. Any idea when the book will be published?"

"Cunningham was really happy about the careful proof reading and said it's almost ready to go after a couple more rounds of editing, which will begin as soon as next week. When I spoke to Steve about it last night, he suggested moving up the date of our wedding. I don't know how I can thank you two enough for introducing me."

"I hope you won't be leaving us too soon," Bobbie said.

"Are you kidding, Bobbie? You, Bob, and Tilly are the family I never had. Besides, I get some of my best writing done right here and at East Hampton. I intend to be around for as long as you want me."

"Bobbie, I think we should take Jane out tonight to celebrate at our to our favorite French restaurant. Mary Petra, the gal who occasionally fills in for Jane, can take care of Tilly."

"I agree, Bob. How about it, Jane? You can invite Steve, your fiancé, to join us."

"Oh, my God. I don't know what I ever did to deserve you two. You're the best."

CHAPTER 47

Bobbie

After breakfast with Jane and Tilly, Bob and I walked to One PP. We were happy as hell about Jane's offer from Random House. I had to fight back tears this morning when Jane said she thinks of us as the family she never had. That's exactly how we think of her—our family. We look forward to our celebration dinner tonight.

Now it's time to lock up some slime balls.

Less than a minute after we walked into our office, Joyce Randolph came bounding in.

"Holy shit," she said, with her increasingly cop-like mouth, "when Bobbie Nelson puts out an APB, people pay attention. That child-kidnapper Adolph Gunther was arrested a half-hour ago and is in the lockup. Mind if I sit in while you interrogate the bastard?"

When Bob, Joyce, and I walked into the interrogation room, Adolph Gunther was seated, shackled to the table by his hands and ankles. Next to him was an attorney we recognized as David Foreman, a well-known criminal lawyer. He knows Bob and me well, and he knows, or should know, that we don't put up with bullshit. I had called Dwight Munson, assistant district attorney, to join the meeting. We want names from this creep, and we know that it will take some plea bargaining to get them.

"Mr. Gunther, you are aware, having been read your rights, that you are under arrest for the kidnapping of a child, specifically a five-year old girl named Tanya Baumgartner. You have been paid a ransom of $100,000 in cash to a bank in the Cayman Islands."

"Objection," Foreman said, "I believe you mean *alleged* kidnapping."

"Little Tanya is prepared to testify as to just how real the *alleged* kidnaping was," I said.

"May we take a brief adjournment and have a chat," Foreman said.

Bob, ADA Munson, Joyce, and I walked into the corridor with David Foreman.

"What, if I may ask, are you folks interested in?" Foreman said. At least this guy's a realist and wants to get right down to plea bargaining.

"Counselor," I said, "As you know we have a photograph taken from his apartment or office, as well as a young victim prepared to testify. Your guy's looking at life without the possibility of parole. 'Open and shut' are the appropriate words to describe this case. *Right now*, and I don't mean five or ten minutes from now, we want the exact locations of the two missing children. If we don't get that, your client will go to solitary confinement, and I will personally supervise his dietary regimen. Do I make myself clear? Nothing negotiable here. Give us those locations—*NOW*."

Sometimes, I admit, I can be a hard ass. And this is one of those times. Gunther knows where those two innocent little kids are, and I want those locations so we can free them.

"I believe Detective Nelson made it quite clear, counselor," ADA Munson chimed in. "Kindly return to the interrogation room, obtain that information, and come back and deliver it to us. *IMMEDIATELY.*"

"I want partial immunity for my client. If he gives you the locations of the children his words cannot be used against him in court," Foreman said.

"Granted," Munson said. "Now make it happen."

CHAPTER 48

D avid Foreman was boxed into a corner and he knew it. So was his client, Adolph Gunther.

But, as that bitchy Detective Nelson pointed out, this case can be described in a simple phrase: *Open and Shut*. He had encountered Detective Bobbie Nelson before, and he had a grudging respect for her professionalism, not to mention her amazing beauty. Although she never practiced, he knew that she was a lawyer, admitted to the bar in Illinois and New York. She graduated near the top of her class from the University of Chicago Law School, and her keen legal mind showed it.

Besides the legal box his client was in, Foreman also knew he had no ethical choice. He needed to get the locations of those two kidnapped kids and give the information to the cops and the prosecutor. Also, he didn't doubt for a minute that Detective Nelson meant it when she said she'd make sure Gunther would be placed in solidarity confinement and that she would control his diet, which would probably consist of bread and water, if that. He really didn't think she was playing by the rules, but the steely look in Nelson's eyes told him she would do it, and bend the rules if she had to.

Foreman had read that Nelson and her husband had recently adopted a baby. He didn't doubt that fact hardened her determination to free the kidnapped kids.

———————

Foreman walked into the interrogation room and sat across from his client.

"Mr. Gunther, you must give me the location of the two missing children."

Foreman seldom spoke to the creeps he represented on a first name basis. Best to keep it formal.

"I do not know," Gunther said in a heavy German accent.

"Mr. Gunther, the parents of those children are wealthy and powerful people. I don't doubt for an instant that they would arrange for you to be assassinated in prison if anything happened to those kids." Foreman had read about kidnapping cases where that is exactly what happened—self-administered justice. And, legal or not, he didn't doubt that Detective Nelson would help facilitate the action. The angry hatred in her eyes made that quite clear.

Gunther wrote down an address in Manhattan.

"Both children are at that address."

"If you called the people at this location would they obey you if you told them to release the children?"

"They would try to escape immediately."

"But if you told them that the police know the location, they would surely know that they would be risking their lives trying to escape."

"My associates are very tough and very determined. I'm afraid that the police must be willing to engage in combat."

"Mr. Gunther, the New York Police Department has a unit called ESU or Emergency Service Unit, the NYPD's equivalent of a SWAT team (Special Weapons and Tactics). They are quite skilled at what they do. I recommend that your colleagues surrender. Let's talk to the detectives and the ADA."

Foreman stuck his head into the hallway and asked them to come inside.

He handed the address where the children were held to ADA Munson. By now Foreman had one objective, one objective only— to protect the children. He realized that the cops and the ADA had the same objective. He knew he had represented his client as best he could. Now it's time for a different role. To save the lives of innocent children.

CHAPTER 49

Bobbie

I called Commissioner Ralph after David Foreman, Gunther's lawyer, gave us the location of the hostage children. I felt respect for Foreman. He did his best for his client and then let his humanity kick in, the humanity of a man with two young children. Ralph walked into the interrogation room and we told him about the situation. I knew exactly what he was about to do, and so did Bob. He called Detective Lieutenant Jillian Pierce, head of the NYPD hostage negotiation unit. Bob and I know about hostage negotiations, having been involved in a few of them as part of investigations. But the people from the hostage negotiation unit are experts at what they do. They're almost like psychologists as they skillfully talk to sometimes panicked and desperate criminals, trying their best to prevent violence against the innocent.

Jillian Pierce herself headed up the team and grabbed her megaphone after first calling the phone number that Adolph Gunther had provided. The Emergency Services Unit was on standby, in case gunplay became inevitable. The phone call was answered, she was happy to see. Talking on the phone is a better way of negotiating than shouting through a megaphone. A woman, who only identified herself as Barbara, answered the phone. Jillian put her phone on speaker so Bob and I could hear. We stood next to her. After prompting, the woman said that a man named Michael was with her. I imagined what if the hostage was our little Tilly, and I was a fucking wreck. I could see that Bob was nervous too.

"Barbara, my name is Detective Pierce, but please call me Jillian. Our objective today is simple, to ensure the safety of everyone involved, and that includes you. The only thing that makes sense at this point is for you and your colleague to release the children and then walk through the front door with your hands up. If you have an attorney, I suggest that you call him or her. If you do not have representation, an attorney will be provided to you. So, what do you say, Barbara?"

Wow, Detective Jillian is one piece of work. I thought I was listening to a couple of old girlfriends shooting the shit.

"Will we be taken into custody?" Barbara asked. Dumb question, I thought. Was she trying to buy time?

"Well, yes," Jillian said softly, "but by ending this situation peacefully, your cooperation will be duly noted. Please let the children walk out first."

After an agonizing minute, two little boys, who we knew were both six years old, suddenly appeared outside the door. They looked scared. A street full of patrol cars can have that effect on people, especially kids. As planned, the boys were sent in my direction. They both hugged me as I gently hustled them behind a bullet-proof van. We hadn't alerted the boys' folks earlier, believing it best not to complicate the hostage negotiation with nearby parents freaking out. Bob immediately called both couples to let them know their sons were okay. He held the phone away from his ear because of the screaming coming from the other end. Bob told them to meet us at One PP.

Two loud shots rang out from inside the building. Four ESU officers rushed in the front door. Jillian's radio sounded and she pressed the answer button.

"Both kidnappers committed suicide, Detective."

Jillian just shrugged. She had accomplished her objective, to free the little hostages. She really didn't give a shit that the abductors killed themselves.

So, thank God, the operation was successful with both child hostages safely in custody, and two people having decided to rid the world of their evil by committing suicide.

We met the parents at One PP. Joyce Randolph met us at the door and gave each of us a hug. The word emotional doesn't quite describe the scene when parents are reunited with their children. I tried to put on my "tough cop" persona, but it didn't work. I broke down in tears. Bob and I looked at each other and had one of our non-verbal conversations. "Let's go home and hug Tilly," our looks said.

CHAPTER 50

Bob

Bobbie and I had just been through one of the most emotionally trying days since we were partnered—a hostage negotiation involving children. The good news is that it had a happy ending. Well, maybe it wasn't too happy for the kidnappers who committed suicide, but I really didn't care about them. They gave themselves the death penalty.

Jane was sitting across the coffee table from Tilly, giving her a chess lesson. Jane is amazing. She's recognized that Tilly is extremely bright, and she constantly challenges her mind.

Bobbie picked up Tilly and hugged her. Then she handed her to me.

"Daddy, that hurts," Tilly said. I guess my hug took on a strength of its own. All I could think about during that hostage negotiation was Tilly.

Little Lucky clearly showed that he wanted a hug too, jumping up and down my leg. I put him on my lap.

Bobbie and I told Jane all about our crazy day. I had to constantly remind Bobbie not to refer to the kidnappers as "evil fucks." We've been diligently trying to keep our environment cussword-free when around Tilly. Lucky is pitching in. As Jane had trained him, every time he hears the words fuck or shit, he barks.

When we told Jane about the happy reunion of parents and kidnapped children at One PP, she started to cry.

"There's so much evil in this world," Jane said, sniffling. "Thank God the BBs were on the case."

She then picked up Tilly and hugged her.

"I've got some fabulous news for you guys," Jane said when she stopped crying. "Steve has taken a job as an assistant professor of finance at the Greenwich Village Campus of NYU. So, you don't need to worry about me moving to Westchester when Steve and I get married. We'll be looking for an apartment right near here, close to my good buddies and little Tilly."

"Oh my God, that's wonderful," Bobbie said. We had been worried about just that. Losing Jane would be horrible, we both agreed. She's definitely part of our family, and soon Steve will be as well. With all the shit we need to put up with in our profession, at least our family life is great.

"I've got some more good news. My editor at Random House called me and said my book is going to be published next month. *A Gun Too Far* will soon be on the shelves!"

"Great news," I said as I gave her a hug. "Don't forget, Bobbie and I want a signed copy as soon as it's out."

"Of course," Jane said. "You two made it happen."

"Jane, after the shitty day that Bob and I went through, I love all your good news."

Lucky barked.

"Hey, potty mouth," I said.

"Sorry, I meant to say *lousy* day."

"I have two words for all this good news," I said.

"And what would those two words be?" Bobbie asked.

"East Hampton!"

Bobbie and Jane both shouted, "Yesss!"

Lucky rolled over onto her back, obviously looking for a tummy scratch. Tilly laughed and clapped her hands. She loves the sound of East Hampton.

I called Commissioner Ralph to ask for a few days off and asked if Joyce Randolph could join us. "Of course," Ralph said. "Well deserved. Go forth and chill."

I called Joyce to invite her and her husband, Mike. Going to East Hampton is getting to be like a caravan. I love that, and so does Bobbie.

CHAPTER 51

Bobbie

Bob and I agree on most things and going to our house in East Hampton is definitely one of them. It's a good thing our house is large, because we seem to be inviting more and more people to join us. We love it. Our good friends and extended family, and a house big enough to fit them all.

I didn't want to rain on our happy parade, so I didn't say anything about that creep who keeps walking by our house. I didn't say anything, but I thought about it.

As we pulled up to the house on Saturday morning, Maggie, our Golden Retriever neighbor, came charging over to greet us. She put her front paws next to the passenger side window. If dogs could talk, I'm sure we'd hear, "Where's Lucky?"

Joyce and Mike Randolph were already there, lounging by the pool. Jane was with us, and her fiancé, Steve would come by later.

Tilly was laughing and clapping. I think Jane does wonderful things for our daughter's outlook on life.

I was about to call a local restaurant to deliver supper for tonight, but Jane wouldn't hear of it. She's a fabulous cook, and I was happy she volunteered. I should really take some cooking lessons from her. In exchange I can teach her how to make reservations.

At 5 p.m. Steve, Jane's fiancé pulled up. Bob put out a few bottles of wine and some booze on the bar. He walked over to me. "Martini, honey?"

"No thanks," I said.

"Hey, we're off work, are you sure you don't want a martini?"

"Thanks, but I really don't feel like it." Bob gave me a confused look. He knows I enjoy a martini when relaxing.

We all pitched in putting the food on the table. Tilly sat in the highchair next to me and proceeded to fling food across the table. Jane gave her a gentle hug and softly told her to stop throwing food. The fare was chicken thighs, mushrooms, peas, brown rice, and quinoa. Nobody, but nobody, prepares chicken like Jane.

Bob stood and proposed a toast. "To good friends and family." Everybody clapped. I raised my glass of Perrier. He looked at me. "Are you sure you don't want a martini?"

"I'm fine, honey."

Jane walked over to the sideboard and grabbed a large shopping bag she had put there. I had been wondering what it was. She reached in and came out with a hardcover book. "This is a review copy, but it will be the same when published. I have a signed copy for each of you. *A Gun Too Far* will soon hit the stands." The room erupted into happy bedlam.

"I even have a copy for Tilly."

I recalled all of the exciting sex scenes in the book and gave Jane a look of concern.

"Don't worry, Bobbie. I'll give Tilly her copy in a few years."

The next morning, Bob was still sleeping, and I was in the bathroom, throwing up. He tapped on the bathroom door and said, "Are you okay honey? It sounded like you were getting sick. Something didn't agree with you?"

I brushed my teeth for the umpteenth time and hopped into the shower. When I came out, Bob was standing there in his robe, looking concerned.

"Is everything okay, baby?"

"Yes," I said, smiling. "Everything is more than okay. It's called 'morning sickness.' I'm pregnant."

One of my favorite things in life is having Bob's arms around me, his big strong arms. He didn't disappoint me. We just stood there, hugging and loving each other. Bob, my big tough sweet-as-a-kitten cop.

Since we married, Bob and I never practiced birth control, and we kept hoping I'd get pregnant. Maybe we make love *too* much, not giving Bob's sperm a running chance to go far enough. I wondered if my getting pregnant had something to do with adopting Tilly. I can see no scientific reason for it, but I love the thought—our gift to Tilly.

When Bob stopped crying—yes, he was actually crying tears of joy over my announcement, he said, "I guess this explains you're not having a martini last night."

"Yes, it does. Nine months from now I'll join you in a whole pitcher full. Hey, it's time for breakfast."

I was dying to go downstairs to make the announcement to everybody.

When we got downstairs, the gang was sitting around the dining room table and Jane was mixing a batch of scrambled eggs.

Bob raised his coffee mug as if in a toast, put his arm around me and said with a big smile,

"Bobbie's having a baby."

The room went nuts. Everybody stood and filed over to me, taking turns giving me hugs. Our new family. It felt great being surrounded by so much love.

I glanced out at the road. There was that guy we've seen walking by constantly. My pregnancy announcement had turned into an early party, and I didn't want to upset anybody. I did, however, snap another photo of the guy. He definitely gives me the creeps.

I gently kicked Bob's leg and leaned over, gestured toward the road, and whispered, "That's the guy Bob, our maybe stalker."

Bob said he wanted to talk to the man, but I pleaded with him not to upset our fun breakfast. He agreed.

The next day at One PP, I would find out something else to feel creepy about.

CHAPTER 52

Bob

I'm glad we had a great weekend in East Hampton because Commissioner Ralph didn't have anything happy to talk to us about.

Bobbie and I walked into Ralph's office at 8:15, having just had breakfast with Jane and Tilly.

Jane is amazing, and so is Tilly. Jane has been teaching her to play chess, and we were almost stunned to see that Tilly had down all the basic moves. And she's just over two years old! Jane is a gift from God.

Ralph wore a puss, a grimace.

"Wazzup, boss?" Bobbie said, trying to lighten things up.

"Although you two weren't even born at the time, I'm sure you remember the Son of Sam case about that serial killer David Berkowitz."

"Bobbie and I have studied all of the big serial killer cases, including those that happened before we arrived on the scene. As I recall, Berkowitz specialized in killing young women and occasionally young couples. He was also known as the *.44 Caliber Killer* because that's the gun he used in all his murders. Are you telling us there's another character like Berkowitz on the loose?"

"We're not certain, because no two murders were done with the same gun. There have been six young couples killed for a total of 12 victims, 10 in their mid-20s and two in their early 30s. Three couples were married and three were dating. The fact that multiple different weapons were used doesn't really tell us anything, because owning a few guns isn't exactly a magic trick. Your talented young assistant, Joyce Randolph, noticed the similar victim profiles. Thanks to Joyce's research, it looks like we're dealing with a serial killer. She's one sharp detective. I'm glad you recommended that I give her a promotion."

"Where did the murders occur?" Bobbie asked.

"They all happened in New York City, in all five boroughs. Just as in the Son of Sam cases, the couples were parked in a car taking in a view of the scenery or necking. One couple was black, one Asian, the rest Caucasian. None of the bullets were fired from the same gun, but they were all 45-caliber. So, that's what you have to go on—nothing."

"Forty-five caliber?" I said. "A fucking hand-held cannon. This bastard wants to make sure hisvictims die."

———————

"Bob, let's not forget our big announcement," Bobbie said.

"Bobbie's having a baby," I said, feeling as if my heart just took wing.

Ralph took the file he was holding and tossed it on the desk. He walked over and gave each of us bear hugs. I noticed tears in his eyes. Our boss is definitely our friend, our good friend.

After we finished our meeting with Ralph, Bobbie and I went to our office.

"This is disgusting, Bob. Who would want to kill young couples?" Bobbie said. "Hey, Bob, why so pensive?"

"I'm thinking about Joyce and her husband and Jane and her fiancé—young couples. Come to think of it, I guess we're a young couple."

"Yeah," Bobbie said. "A pregnant young couple."

CHAPTER 53

Bobbie

B ob is becoming the Daddy-to-Be on steroids. He won't let me lift anything, and when I go to the ladies' room he asks if everything is okay. I keep reminding him that I'm in excellent physical condition—just pregnant. But he insists on being over-protective of me—and our growing child.

It's impossible not to love this man.

Bob and I spent the rest of the day pouring over the evidence in our latest serial killer case. We had piss poor little evidence to look at. A couple of good-looking young people shot to death and nothing left behind at the crime scene, except for their bodies. The only physical evidence we had were the bullets, but that isn't much help without a gun to match them with. All the murders occurred at night, which was normal because killers don't want to be seen. The difficult thing about serial killer cases is trying to figure out why the killer does what he does. We usually start with the assumption that the killer is a psychopath.

Our old friend, Detective-Psychiatrist Bennie Weinberg just walked into our office. Typical of Bennie, he handed me a bouquet of flowers and gave me a kiss on the cheek. Bob had told him that I'm expecting a baby. Also typical of soft-hearted Bennie, he started to cry after handing me the flowers.

Among his many talents, Bennie is an expert on psychopathy. We reviewed for him the information we had to date.

"Let's start with a working hypothesis that the killer is a psychopath or a sociopath," Bennie said.

He explained to us that there are four types of psychopaths: visionary, mission-driven, hedonistic, and power-seeking.

"A visionary psycho believes he's being spoken to by demons, or maybe even God. He often suffers from hallucinations, and the demons are part of the hallucinations. Son of Sam is a case in point—sort of. Berkowitz originally told investigators that he was responding to the voice of a demon in his head, a dog named Harvey, which belonged to his neighbor, Sam. Most shrinks, myself included, upon hearing that information, diagnosed him as a psychopath. But it subsequently came out that his story was a hoax, and he admitted as much. He was found competent to stand trial. When I first read about the case, I assumed he was a psychopath, but I was wrong. Serial killers can be full of shit.

"A mission-oriented psycho believes he's serving a function to society by removing a perceived evil, such as prostitution or even immigrants. There was one famous case where the killer went after priests. Yes, a mission-driven psycho thinks he's doing good deeds.

"A hedonistic psycho kills for sexual pleasure. Often the only way they can achieve an orgasm is by killing somebody. They're notorious for being sloppy because they're so eager to commit the next murder so they can have the next climax. Can you imagine getting sexual gratification from shooting young people? But as I said before, I don't think this creep is a hedonistic killer, because there's nothing careless or sloppy bout this guy. He's very methodical. Also, there is no evidence of sexual molestation in any of the murders.

"A power or control-seeking nut can also be seen as *thrill killers*. The classic example is the nurse or doctor who kills patients by overdosing them with medications or withholding medication. These are commonly called 'Angel of Death' cases.

"Tell me anything you can about the victim profiles, assuming there *is* a common profile."

"Yeah, we do have a profile," I said. "All of the victims were young couples. Three were married and three were engaged. Also, they were all quite good-looking, although I know that's a subjective opinion." I spread the photos of all the victims, before death, of course.

"I have to agree with your analysis," Bennie said. "They were definitely good-looking people. So, what's your opinion on the type of psycho we're dealing with?"

"I think he's what you called mission-driven," I said. "For reasons we may never know, this creep is on a mission to take the lives of young, good-looking people."

"I agree with Bobbie," Bob said, "the guy seems to be on a mission. But what does that tell us? Is the guy ugly or homely and wants to take revenge on people he wished he could look like? How the hell can we focus an investigation on ugly people? Besides that, some normal-looking people hate the way they look, although they aren't objectively bad-looking."

A look of concern sprouted all over Bennie's face.

"Why the puss, Bennie?" I asked.

"I just realized something, Bobbie. You and Bob are a young

good-looking couple."

"And we're also armed and know how to use our guns," I said. "Don't worry about us, Bennie."

I'll do the worrying for you, I thought.

"This case is starting to remind me of the Son of Sam murders. Recall that Berkowitz, although he would never appear on the cover of *GQ Magazine*, wasn't ugly," Bennie said. "A bit homely perhaps, but definitely not ugly. And, just like Berkowitz, this killer focuses on young good-looking people. But unlike Berkowitz, who always used the same .44 caliber pistol, this killer uses a different gun in each murder. They were all .45 caliber, but never the same gun. That really fucks up your forensic analysis. I know you two pros like to get the job done, and get it done fast, but I'm afraid we'll just have to wait for a lucky break, or a mistake by the killer. As a detective myself, I hate to use the word luck, but we're going to need some luck with this case."

Bob smacked the table with both hands. He obviously just had a big thought.

"Two words just occurred to me," Bob said. *"Lovers' lane.* I think we all know what that means: a secluded area with parking and maybe a nice view, a place where young lovers can make out or maybe even screw in the back seat. The Zodiac killer in California was fond of killing in places like that, and a few of the Berkowitz victims were killed in such spots."

"Leave it to my romantic partner to come up with this idea," I said, laughing. "But I think Bob is spot on as usual. A lovers' lane is an ideal spot for the killer to do his work. Hell, from our victim profiles, every couple was murdered in a car and the location could be described as a lovers' lane."

"I think we should turn loose our brilliant assistant detective on this—Joyce Randolph," Bob said. "Maybe her research will show us the most popular lovers' lanes in the city. Once we narrow down the lovers' lanes to the popular ones, we can hang a surveillance camera focusing on the parking area. Maybe we'll get lucky."

"When I listen to you two I know why you're such famous detectives," Bennie said. "I think your surveillance camera idea on lovers' lanes is brilliant, Bob. Go for it, my friends."

CHAPTER 54

Bob

As soon as Bennie left, I buzzed Joyce and asked her to come to our office. She had recently been promoted from junior detective to full Detective Third Grade, largely thanks to recommendations from Bobbie and me. At her specific request, Commissioner Ralph agreed to assign Joyce to work cases with us, rather than give her a partner. We've become good friends with Joyce and her husband, Mike. Bobbie and I often give her the keys to our vacation house in East Hampton, to give her more reason to renew her request to keep working with us. I've never seen anybody research the Internet better than Joyce. Mike may be her husband, but Google is her lover.

We explained what we were after, a list of the most popular lovers' lanes in the city, places where we'd insert surveillance cameras.

"What a fabulous fucking idea," Joyce said, with her ever expanding cop-mouth. "That's why I love working with the BBs. This is going to take a lot of subjective searching, because I doubt that *Zagat's* has come out with a rating system for lovers' lanes. But I don't doubt for a minute that some enterprising magazine or newspaper reporters have looked at this as an interesting story. I'll feed you the locations as I come up with them, rather than wait until we have a full list.

She was right. More than one magazine reporter thought it was a good story. She found a long article in a Sunday *New York Times* entitled, "New York City's Favorite Lovers' Lanes." The article listed no fewer than 22 locations. I called Commissioner Ralph and he assigned two sharp junior detectives to place the cameras, people with experience in surveillance work. In addition to the cameras, the detectives would install audio listening devices that were specifically tuned to alert One PP if it picked up the sound of a gunshot. When they did the installations, they would be dressed as electrical workers to keep their covers on tight.

Within five days, Joyce had come up with a list of 26 popular lovers' lanes, 22 from the *New York Times* article and four from other news stories. So far, 20 surveillance cameras have been installed, and the rest scheduled for today.

CHAPTER 55

Bobbie

B ob's idea of installing surveillance cameras at popular lover's lanes was typically brilliant. The idea isn't foolproof—hell, nothing in detective work is foolproof. The thinking is that the serial killer would haunt lover's lanes just as lovers do. If you want to find lovers, or kill them, go to the places where lovers like to hang out. As the famed bank robber Willie Sutton said when asked why he robbed banks, he said, "Because that's where the money is." Bob knows his stuff.

Last night there was another murder of a handsome young couple. It occurred at a popular lovers' lane in Queens. The place was on Joyce's database, but unfortunately the surveillance camera hadn't been installed yet. It was scheduled for today. The only positive thing about this senseless killing was that it confirmed Bob's theory about lovers' lanes.

Another week went by, and we were both nervous as hell. The killer has seemed to adopt a schedule of one murder per week. That would mean that there will be another murder of an attractive young couple tonight. The forecast is for moderate to heavy rain through tonight, an ideal time for a killing because that would mean fewer couples would be parked, and there would be fewer witnesses. I can't wait to nail this bastard.

It was 9 p.m., and we had just put Tilly to bed. Bob and I sat in the den watching TV. The phone rang. It was Joyce. I put her on speaker.

"Another shooting, this one less than five minutes ago. The listening device worked perfectly and alerted One PP. I just downloaded the video. Why don't you log onto our Intranet and watch it with me? It happened at a popular lover's lane just off the Belt Parkway overlooking the Verrazano Bridge."

Bob and I logged in and watched the video. The technology is amazing.

A tall Caucasian man climbed out of his beige Toyota Land Cruiser and casually walked over to the other car in the parking lot. The rain had slowed down, and there was only a slight drizzle. He walked to the passenger side door and fired four rounds into the BMW. It was sickening to know that two people had just been killed—and we saw it happen. He turned, giving us an excellent view of his face.

"Holy shit, Bob. You know who he looks like?"

"Yeah, our strolling friend from East Hampton."

We also had a clear view of the license plate number on his car— QZ-1279. He then got back into his SUV and drove off at a moderate speed, heading east on the Belt Parkway.

I asked Joyce to switch me to the communications department and I immediately put out an APB for a "beige Toyota Land Cruiser bearing the plate number QZ-1279, last seen heading east on the Belt Parkway, driven by a Caucasian male approximately six feet tall. The man is armed and dangerous." I told Joyce to make sure the still photo of the guy was attached to the APB.

I cannot fucking believe that this guy is our East Hampton stalker, the man who walks by our house constantly. And who was there last weekend? Three young couples, Jane and Steve, Joyce and Mike— and Bob and me. I looked at the guy's photo I had taken on my phone, then looked at the shot of lovers' lane from our surveillance camera.

It's him.

Bob called Commissioner Ralph on his cellphone and let him know what was happening. I was sure we'd collar the guy. I think I put everything I possibly could on my APB, including a description of the vehicle, its license plate number and a photo of the man. And he was driving on a well-known parkway.

Then I called Joyce's office at One PP, guessing that she may still be there.

"Hey, Joyce, what the heck are you doing at One PP at this time of night?"

"Mike's away at a conference, so I figured I'd catch up on things."

"Catch up you did, my friend. Did you ever."

CHAPTER 56

D avid Muir for *ABC World News Tonight,* ladies and gentlemen. We have just received a report that the NYPD has apprehended a suspect in that recent horrible spate of serial killings of young couples. He was arrested a half-hour ago on the Belt Parkway where it merges with the Southern State. The road is closed, and east-bound traffic is at a complete standstill.

"From the report we've heard, the man opened fire on one of the officers but fortunately missed him. The bullet shattered the windshield of the patrol car. After a brief struggle, the man was apprehended. He is now in custody at the lockup at police headquarters.

"The man was caught on video firing his gun into a car at a parking area on the Belt Parkway in Brooklyn about 20 minutes before he was arrested. I'm sad to say that the occupants of the car were a young couple in their 20s. They were pronounced dead at the scene. This murder brings the total number of young people killed to 24. They were all young couples, either married or engaged. Let's hope that the police have the right guy.

"In other news…"

CHAPTER 57

Bob

W hen Bobbie nails it, she nails it. Her quick-thinking APB resulted in the arrest of the suspect 20 minutes after she put it out. Bobbie moves fast. And I'm still trying to come to grips with the fact that the serial killer is the same man who constantly walks by our house in East Hampton.

We were just finishing breakfast with Jane and Tilly. Jane, our pretty young governess, along with her handsome fiancé Mike, would have been the perfect targets for this slime who is now in custody. That alone made me happy we caught the bastard. Come to think of it, Joyce and Mike, not to mention Bobbie and I would make good targets as well. And, the bastard was stalking our house in East Hampton.

Bobbie excused herself and went to the ladies' room for a bout of morning sickness. It' been happening less frequently in the past few days. Typical of positive-thinking Bobbie, she tells me it doesn't really bother her, and that it's a happy reminder that our new child on the way. Only Bobbie could see vomiting as a good thing.

When we walked into Commissioner Ralph's office he stood and gave us both bear hugs. "You've done it again, BBs, God bless you. Bob, your idea of surveillance cameras on lovers' lanes was simple brilliance. And Bobbie's APB enabled us to grab the bastard within minutes. I'll never get over saying this, but *job well done*."

"Bobbie and I are planning to interrogate the prisoner shortly, Ralph. Can you tell us anything about him?" Although Bobbie and I are certain we know who the man is, I wanted some background from Ralph for our interrogation.

"Get ready for a shock, guys. His name is David McCallister, PhD. He's a full professor of literature at Columbia University. He's divorced three times and has no kids. When not murdering young couples and teaching classes, he runs the debate team at Columbia. He graduated first in his class from Harvard and got his PhD at Yale. Not your typical serial killer. A search warrant is being executed at his apartment as we speak. Have at it, BBs, we'll know a lot more about this guy after you interrogate him."

Then I shared with Ralph our thinking that this is a man who constantly stalks our vacation house in East Hampton. Ralph looked stunned.

"He's represented by counsel, I assume," Bobbie said.

"No, another surprise. He refused his right to make the phone call and he refused to have assigned counsel. Dr. McAllister is one strange fucking dude."

As Bobbie and I walked to the interrogation room, I turned to her and said, "This is likely to be emotional, hon. Do you think it may bring on a bout of morning sickness?"

"I hope it does, Bob. I'll be happy to puke in that bastard's face."

When Bobbie and I walked into the interrogation room, McAllister sat at the table shackled by his ankle and wrists. When we first started investigating the case, we both assumed that the killer would be ugly, or at least homely, and that's why he attacked and killed young good-looking people. But, now that we're seeing him up close for the first time, this guy could only be described as handsome. According to his intake sheet he was 53 years old and ran marathons as a hobby. His black hair was streaked with hints of gray. His steel blue eyes freaked me out. It may sound crazy, but he had the eyes of a killer. I also noticed that he gave Bobbie a thorough going over with those leering eyes. I had the unsettling thought that he was considering how he'd enjoy killing her—and me. We agreed that Bobbie would begin the interrogation.

"Mr. McAllister, I have one major question," Bobbie said.

"I believe you mean *Doctor* McAllister."

I could tell she wanted to punch him as much as I did, but nobody is cooler when it comes to interrogating repulsive creeps than Bobbie, no matter what their title. She didn't want to argue with him. *Never* argue with an interrogee.

"Fine, *Doctor* McAllister. My major question is this: Why did you do this?"

"And by the word *this*, to what are you referring? I am a professor, and I'm accustomed to speaking in precise terms."

I always admire Bobbie's patience when dealing with difficult interrogees.

"By *this*, I am referring to the 24 people you murdered. Why did you do it?"

"It? Singular?"

"Okay," Bobbie said, exhaling a breath. "Why did you do those things, kill those people?"

"Well, nobody lives forever, now, do they?"

There was a knock on the door. It was Detective Tim Connolly, the man who was in charge of executing the search warrant on McAllister's apartment.

"Can I speak to one of you?"

Since Bobbie was continuing her interrogation, I stepped into the hallway with Detective Tim.

"You cannot fucking believe the number of weapons we found in this guy's apartment, Bob. I haven't seen so many guns in one place since I was in the Army. Every type of handgun imaginable and at least 10 semi-automatic rifles. It's a fucking arsenal. I figured I should let you know because I'm sure you'll want to question him about the guns in your interrogation."

"Thanks, Tim. At times like this I find myself wishing we had the death penalty in New York."

I walked back into the interrogation room.

Bobbie was still playing word games with the punctilious Dr. McAllister. She looked at me as if to say, "Got something to add?"

"How many guns do you own, including handguns and rifles?" I said.

"How do you know I own guns?"

"That man I just spoke to is the detective in charge of executing the search warrant on your apartment. He described it as looking like an arsenal."

"Oh, that's only a few of them. I have many more at my house in East Hampton."

"We'll need you to provide us with the address of your house in East Hampton."

"It's nothing as resplendent as yours, but it's comfortable."

"You're familiar with our house?" I said. I figured I'd not let on that we knew it was him—just yet.

"Yes, quite familiar with it. Commissioner Norquist also has a nice place, right near mine. I've noticed that you often entertain good-looking young couples. You two are also an attractive young couple."

I nodded to Bobbie to keep going. I needed to take few breaths and concentrate on not punching this guy's lights out. I'm sure he was fantasizing about killing Bobbie and me, not to mention Jane and her fiancé, and Joyce and her husband. I had the sinking feeling that Jane was absolutely right—this guy was stalking us, no doubt planning to kill us.

"Getting back to my previous question, Dr. McAllister, why did you murder those people? Your response was that nobody lives forever. That's true, of course, but why does that mean you felt you needed to take their lives yourself?"

"If not me, who?"

"So, you *did* murder those 24 people?"

"Yes."

Bobbie just got the guy to clearly admit to 24 cases of first-degree murder. She knows what she's doing. We looked at each other and had one of our wordless conversations. Our looks said that we were done with this creep—for today.

We went to Ralph's office and told him all about our interrogation, which was videotaped.

"Why am I not surprised that you got him to admit to the murders? I'm sure the DA will look for 24 life sentences to be served consecutively. This animal will never see the outside world again. Way to go, BBs."

I then told Ralph about his house in East Hampton, right near Ralph's, and also about his detailed knowledge of our house. Nice feeling to know that you were being stalked by a serial killer.

So, we solved the case, and Doctor McAllister will spend the rest of his life in prison. At least he has a life, unlike the 24 young people he murdered.

Bobbie and I felt relaxed and happy that we nailed the prick. What we didn't know was that a phone call that night would put us into middle of some more shit, more than I could ever have imagined.

CHAPTER 58

Bobbie

Bob and I felt great about putting an end to McAllister's killing spree. The professor will spend the rest of his life in prison, and he will no longer stalk our house in East Hampton. We walked into our apartment at 5:30. Steve Rankin, Jane's fiancé, was away at a two-day conference, so we invited Jane to have dinner with Bob, Tilly, and me and to stay over. She had just started on a new novel. We love to have Jane over for meals, not just because we enjoy her company, but because she's a fabulous cook.

We told Jane all about our serial killer case, including the fact that he had been the man stalking our house in East Hampton. We didn't want to upset her but thought it a good idea to remind her to always be on the lookout.

"Oh my God," Jane said. "When I close my eyes, I can see his leering face. I guess you don't need to be a detective to assume he was planning on killing all of us."

"Yes," I said, "that's the conclusion I try to forget about."

The phone rang, and I looked at caller ID. Most of the calls to our landline phone are from telemarketers so I usually don't answer. But this was from a hospital in Florida so I figured I should pick it up.

It was Tim Lawton, Bob's 17-year-old nephew. I put him on speaker.

"Please put Uncle Bob on," he said.

"I'm right here, Tim," Bob said. "I notice that you're calling from a hospital in Florida. Is everything okay?"

"I've got a problem, Uncle Bob, a big problem."

"You sound different, Tim."

"I've got a broken nose, that's probably why I sound different."

"Okay, tell me everything, Tim," Bob said, a look of concern on his face. Bob is fond of his nephew and Tim worships his Uncle Bob.

"Uncle Bob, I need your help. I'm down here in Florida for an anniversary party for a friend's parents. I had a few too many drinks and was driving back to the place I was staying when I was pulled over. I blew a .09 on the breathalyzer and the legal limit is .08, and I got hit with a felony DUI. I'm calling you from a lockup unit in the hospital."

"Were you in an accident, Tim?" Bob said.

"Yeah, I nodded off and crashed into a woman's car. I got a broken nose and a fractured arm. I understand that the woman had a fractured wrist and a bad shoulder injury. Her car is totally wrecked. Uncle Bob, please don't mention a word of this to my dad."

"Do you have lawyer?" Bob asked, paying no attention to his plea not to speak to his father.

"Yeah, they gave me a court-appointed lawyer. His name is James

Griffin. Here's his number. He's expecting to hear from you. I told him I was sure you'd help me out."

"I'll call him right now. I'll call you on your cellphone and let you know what he says."

"My cellphone was confiscated. You can't call me here at the hospital, so I'll call you tomorrow. Good night, Uncle Bob and Aunt Bobbie."

"I cannot friggin believe this," Bob said. "Tim is a good kid, as good as you can get for a 17-year-old. This is one goddam mess."

"I should go," Jane said. "This is none of my business."

"Please stay put, Jane," Bob said. "Do I need to remind you that we consider you family?"

"And while you're staying put, why don't you whip up some of that wonderful crème brulee of yours," I said, trying to lighten up the tension in the room. "Bob, go ahead and call that Florida lawyer, although it's after seven, so he's probably gone home by now."

Bob called the number.

"Miami Legal Aid Society" said the person who answered the phone. "How may I assist you?"

"May I please speak to a lawyer named James Griffin?" Bob said. The call was put through. We were surprised that Griffin picked up even though it was getting late. I guess legal aid lawyers are used to putting in long hours.

"Jim Griffin here. What can I do for you?"

"My name is Bob Lawton. I'm a detective with the NYPD. I'm here with my wife, Bobbie who is a lawyer besides being my detective partner. Please call us Bob and Bobbie. I understand that you are representing my nephew, Timothy Lawton."

"Yes, I have been assigned to your nephew's case. That young man is in a lot of trouble. He's been hit with a felony DUI charge, and he was involved in an accident in which a woman was seriously injured."

"What happened to the woman?" Bob asked.

"Fractured wrist—her right wrist, which is dominant, and a fractured left shoulder. She's a hairdresser and is disabled from returning to work."

"Have you been in touch with Tim's insurance company?" Bob asked.

"Your nephew is uninsured, for which he received another citation. But Ms. Johnson seems to be a pleasant and non-confrontational person. She's willing to settle for $40,000 in exchange for which she won't press charges. The assistant district attorney agreed. So, $40,000 and young Tim will be released with no criminal record. Tim told me that you will help him, Bob. Not a bad deal if you ask me."

"How shall I pay this?" Bob asked.

"A certified check should be made payable to Ms. Gwendolyn Johnson. Send it to me and I will give it to her in exchange for a full release. Please send it to my home address because the county doesn't like public defenders to get involved in financial transactions. As soon as Ms. Johnston receives the check, your nephew will be released. You may want to overnight the check."

"I'll take care of it first thing in the morning," Bob said. He hung up and looked at me.

"Something's wrong here," I said. "Call your brother right now."

"But Tim begged me not to tell him."

"But you didn't agree to anything. Call Mike right now, Bob. He's your brother for Chrissake."

Bob put the phone on speaker and dialed his brother.

"Hello."

Bob and I looked at each other. That voice sounded just like Tim.

"Tim?"

"Hi Uncle Bob. Wow, I just read about that huge murder case that you and Aunt Bobbie solved. You guys are the best."

"Tim, is that you?"

"Of course, it's me. What's up, Uncle Bob?"

"Are your mom and dad nearby? If so, put the phone on speaker so I can talk to all three of you."

"Hi, Bob. I'm here with Amy. How's everything?" Mike said.

"I just got off the phone with a guy calling from a hospital in Miami. He said he was Tim Lawton and sounded a lot like him. He said he had a broken nose from a car accident for which he received a felony DUI and needed help. He gave me the number of his court appointed lawyer, who said the person he crashed into was injured and is willing to settle for $40,000. He said he didn't have insurance. The lawyer said I should send a certified check to his office and he would give it to the woman."

"Hey, Bob. You and Bobbie are the two sharpest detectives in the country. Don't you smell a rat? Tim is standing next to me and he doesn't have a broken nose. And we're in Brooklyn, not Miami."

"And I have insurance," Tim said.

"Yeah, Mike, I smell more than a rat. Bobbie and I have some work to do. I'll let you know when we find something. Great to hear your voice, Tim."

"This is obviously a scam, Bob," I said. "I can't believe an attorney is involved in this. Let's check him out."

Bob sat in front of the computer and typed in the search string, "James Griffin attorney Florida." The result showed one attorney in Miami named James Griffin and that he specialized in estate planning. The phone number was different from the one Bob had been given by that mysterious Tim character. Bob called the number but got an answering machine. It's 7:30 p.m. so that was no surprise. We'd call in the morning. We invited Jane to stay overnight.

———————

The next morning at nine, Bob again called the number of the attorney James Griffin. The receptionist put Bob through to Griffin.

"James Griffin here, how may I help you?"

"Jim, you sound different from the guy I spoke to last night," Bob said.

"Who are you?"

"I'm Bob Lawton a detective with the NYPD. I spoke to a lawyer named James Griffin last night. He was at the Miami Legal Aid Office."

"There's no such organization, Bob. I'm afraid you've been scammed, my friend, although this is the first time I've heard my name used. The entire Florida bar knows about these people, which is why they usually prey on out-of-state people like you. Let me guess. You got a call from a teenager posing as a relative of yours, saying he'd been in a car accident and gave you the name of a fictitious lawyer. My guess is that the kid said he had a broken nose, and that's why he sounded different. You called the lawyer and he tried to hit you up for as much as $50,000 to settle the case with the woman he supposedly crashed into. Does that sound familiar?"

"Yes, that's exactly what happened," Bob said. "The settlement amount was $40,000 and I was supposed to send a certified check overnight to the phony lawyer. Thank you for your help. If I find out anything, I'll let you know. And if you hear anything about a teenager named Tim Lawton, I'd appreciate it if you'd let me know. He's my nephew and he wasn't in Florida when I received the scam call from a person pretending to be him."

"I'll definitely let you know if I hear anything. Welcome to the Sunshine State, Bob."

CHAPTER 59

Bobbie

B ob was upset about almost being scammed, and who can blame him? I'm pissed off myself. If he hadn't called his brother, and spoken to his real nephew, we would have sent a certified check for $40,000 to the thieves the next day.

We were sitting in our office, having just had breakfast with Jane and Tilly. I had a very brief bout of morning sickness.

"Hey, Bob, why so pensive? Let's just put that shit behind us."

"Maybe this job is getting to me, Bobbie. I usually think of myself as a positive thinker, but the crap we constantly deal with makes it hard to be positive. Words keep rattling around my brain, words I wish I could let go of. I hear guns, bullets, dead bodies, murder, blood, injuries, fraud, and scams. I hear those words all the time. They just keep buzzing around my brain. I don't know how you can maintain such a positive outlook on life. You're amazing, Bobbie."

I stood, walked around the desk, and wrapped my arms around

Bob's shoulders. Then I kissed him on the ear.

"Honey, listen to me. Forget those words rattling around in your head. There are only three magical words I think about constantly—three magical words that keep all that crap in perspective."

"And what are those three magical words?"

"I love you."

Characters – *Puzzles Book 2*

Andrews, Marilyn – President of the Senior Council

Basak, Aarav – Internet scam artist

Bateman, Jenny – CEO, Robot Depot

Billings, Frank – Major, US Army Corps of Engineers

Browner, Henry (Hank) – MTA investigator

Buster – Director of the CIA, aka, Charles Atkins

Durmand, Max - Army colonel and prison commandant

Flynn, Tom – Subway passenger

Foreman, David – Attorney for kidnapper

Hiral, Aditya – Internet scam artist

Lawton, Bob - NYPD Detective, Bobbie's partner

Lawton, Mike – Bob's brother

Lawton, Tim – Bob's nephew

Mason, George – General manager, MetLife Stadium

Munir, Ali – Terrorist prisoner

Mussin, Ali – Terrorist and handyman at MetLife Stadium

Nelson, Bobbie – NYPD Detective, Bob's partner

Paxton, Arnold – Mayor of New York City

Quintal, Hugo – Court appointed attorney for an Internet scammer

Randolph, Joyce – Junior detective and assistant to Bob and Bobbie

Randolph, Mike – Joyce's husband

Romelli, Jane – Babysitter and novelist

Rankin, Steve– Jane Romelli's fiancé

Reynolds, Evelyn – Restaurant owner

Spencer, Bob – Internet scam artist

Tiverton, Molly – NYC Commissioner of Transportation

Townsend, Mike – Suffolk County Police Commissioner

Tucker, Wayne – Brigadier General, US Army Electronics Warfare

The Books of Russ Moran

All books are available on Amazon.com, and also as ebooks on The Kindle or a Kindle app on your smartphone or iPad.

The Gray Ship – **Book One of** *The Time Magnet Series*
http://amzn.to/16GPumH

"This provocative, intensely powerful novel is a must-read for sci-fi fans and Civil War aficionados, though mainstream fiction readers will find it heart-rending and inspiring as well. A rare read that's not only wildly entertaining, but also profoundly moving." — Kirkus Reviews

The Thanksgiving Gang – **Book Two of** *The Time Magnet Series*
http://amzn.to/1NzBs7N

The Sequel to *The Gray Ship.* A story of time travel.

"I had never read a book before written in an efficient, minimalistic prose. Instead of writing what most readers want to read, he gives voice to life-like characters, with their flaws and prejudices. They are not infallible superheroes. It's always nice to find a new voice in fiction and to enjoy creativity at its best." — C. Ludewig.

"Breakneck pacing and virtually nonstop action" – Kirkus Reviews

A Time of Fear – **Book Three of** *The Time Magnet Series*
http://amzn.to/1zdjaG9

In a month, five American cities will be devastated by suitcase nuclear bombs.

The time travelers take on their old name, *The Thanksgiving Gang.*

-They know what will happen, because they travelled to the future.

-They know what the result will be. They've seen the devastation.

-They know the details. Five American Cities targeted by nuclear suitcase bombs.

-BUT they don't know where the bombs are—and they don't know how to find them.

The clock is ticking, and millions will soon lose their lives – unless they find the bombs.

"His story is fascinating, and adds even more depth to this already cavernously deep novel. Amazingly unique, chilling and well written, Moran weaves a future that is both desperate and hopeful. Blending modern fears with science fiction results in a tale that will keep you reading long into the night. Five stars!" – Heather

The Skies of Time – **Book Four of** *The Time Magnet Series*
http://amzn.to/1CCC3jg

In *The Skies of Time*, you will recognize the two main characters, Ashley Patterson, now an admiral, and her husband, Jack Thurber. They met and fell in love in *The Gray Ship*, and now they're in for the adventure of their lives in *The Skies of Time*. Ashley and Jack have been such prominent characters in all four books of The Time Magnet Series that I feel like they're old friends. You will also recognize some of the other characters. But if I told you who they are, it would ruin the fun.

"I'm big fan of this series and this one may be the best. I hope there is another book to this series since it keeps getting better. There are a few questions I have about certain events that makes the next one even more suspenseful. These are great books to binge read one after the other." — Time Travel Fan

The Shadows of Terror – Book One of the *Patterns Series*
http://amzn.to/1IDQzJS

A novel that explodes off the front page of your newspaper.

Terrorism has a new face, a face that's obscured in the shadows. The radical forces of destruction have learned to make themselves invisible to the West, and preventing a terrorist attack has become almost impossible.

A new war has begun, World War III.

Rick Bellamy, an FBI agent who specializes in counterterrorism, is engaged in his own war, a war with no end.

Bellamy's wife, Ellen, a prominent architect, discovers that she's in the middle of the greatest terror plot to date.

To defeat the enemy, Bellamy first has to uncover the clues, to shine a light on the shadows. He has to find patterns – before it's too late.

"Move over James Patterson and Mary Higgins Clark. There's a new guy in town. Russ Moran's new book – *The Shadows of Terror*." — Frank O.

The Scent of Revenge - **Book Two in the *Patterns Series*.**
http://amzn.to/1UvDRmw

The world is at war with the forces of terror. FBI Agent Rick Bellamy and his wife, Ellen, find themselves in the middle of a sinister terrorist plot.

Someone is attacking young prominent women, inflicting a horrible disease.

Nobody knows its origin, nobody knows how to stop it, nobody knows how to cure it.

Rick Bellamy and a team of scientists want to go on the offense. But how?

Will the lives of the women be changed forever? When will the attacks stop?

"Heart pounding, can't put down thriller that will force you to look at terrorism in different light. Life in America will never be the same." – Cold Coffee Cafe

Sideswiped - **Book One in the Matt Blake series of legal thrillers.** http://amzn.to/1MkxX35

Trial lawyer Matt Blake took on a perfect case.

It involved a sideswipe collision in which his client's husband, an investigative reporter, was killed. The evidence of negligence was overwhelming. Eyewitnesses testified that defendant was talking on his cell phone when he hit the other car.

But was it negligence? Was it an accident?

Or was it murder?

Matt uncovers evidence that the act may have been intentional. Somebody wanted the man silenced. Somebody wanted the man dead.

Somebody had a lot to hide.

The signs started to point to the highest levels of government.

An open-and-shut personal injury case suddenly became a vast conspiracy of terror.

"This book hooks you in from the first line. *Sideswiped* draws you into the world of Matt Blake and you become emotionally attached to him and his journey. The story itself is so well-written and moves quickly. There is never a dull moment." —Sarah Elle

"Moran demonstrates the depth of his writing talent by developing a new genre with *Sideswiped*, a legal thriller. Branching out from his previous novels dealing with time travel, Moran goes in a whole new direction with Book One in the Matt Blake series. He creates a wild but totally believable story of modern day intrigue and suspense. Moran also deftly weaves into this book some of my favorite characters from his prior novels. I am looking forward to starting Book #2 - *The Reformers* — Frank from Lynbrook on August 16, 2016

The Reformers - **Book Two of the Matt Blake Series of legal thrillers, is the sequel to** *Sideswiped.*
http://amzn.to/2m8uMdu

The forces of radical Islam are on the run.

Their leadership has been decimated, their ranks thinned, their power disappearing by the week.

Their recruiting efforts have been cut off, the radical websites shut down, and the attraction of jihad is losing its appeal among the young.

With targeted assassinations, military strikes, as well as the loss of oil fields and gold mines, radical Islam is fast losing power.

But who is responsible?

It isn't the United States Government. It's a new force the world has never seen before.

Lawyer Matt Blake and his wife Diana find themselves in the middle of the most gigantic plot the world has ever seen, a conspiracy that's only begun to grow.

"I've been a fan of the author, Russell Moran, since reading *Sideswiped* a few months ago, so I admittedly went into this book with quite high expectations. That being said, I had no idea that "*The Reformers*" was going to play out in the way that it does and I can see myself giving this book a re-read in the future. In fact, I am even more impressed by the storyline of this read than the last and it has left me excited to see more." – Lucidity.

The Keepers of Time – **Book Five of the Time Magnet Series**
http://amzn.to/2wjVSTt

Admiral Ashley Patterson and her husband Jack have done it again. They've traveled through time, 200 years into the future—aboard a nuclear aircraft carrier, Ashley's flagship.

They discover a new world, a strange new world—a post-nuclear war world—one that is both a beacon of hope, and a cry of despair.

They meet a group of people who call themselves *The Keepers of Time,* an organization dedicated to preserving history and culture amid the horrors of a dystopian future.

The world around them has harkened back to a primitive and savage past, one that includes human sacrifice.

Ashley knows they must have to get back to the present to warn the government of the unspeakable horrors that await. But finding the way back to the present is their greatest challenge, an almost insurmountable one.

"The Keepers of Time is a really interesting take on current geopolitical events and where they are leading. From reading previous books in the series, the cast of characters is as familiar as the people next door and it was great to reconnect with them. Moran's legal background illuminates what happens when our legal structure disappears, and he has zeroed in on an essential thing about civilization -- records of the past. A great read!" Robert Shearer

"Time flies when you're scared out of your mind. The author's superb writing skills will quickly draw you into the story. Forty two fast paced chapters will keep turning the pages of this novel until the end. Well-developed cast of realistic characters that you will relate to one will keep you engaged. One of my favorite things about Moran's books is his entire cast of characters detailed in the back of the book. I admit to reading about the cast first in order to firmly get everyone in my mind. As a follower of his, I know each character is important to the plot and I don't want to miss anything or overlook anyone." – Cold Coffee

"A wild time travel yarn that starts fast and doesn't slow down until the end."

A Reunion in Time
http://amzn.to/2tneIsg

What if a 37-year-old adult travels back 20 years in time and finds himself in high school, followed by his 36-year-old wife? They're now teenagers, 17 and 16.

Adults in teenage bodies, they struggle to convince the people from their past that they are real, not apparitions. With the benefit of hindsight, they know the history of the past 20 years, and it isn't pretty.

Rick and Ellen are married, and now have to adjust to married life as teenagers in 2001. Rick is a senior FBI official and Ellen is a famous architect.

But everybody sees them as kids. Nobody believes that they're married, and nobody believes their stories—until Rick and Ellen predict 9/11.

How do they find their way back to the year they came from? How do they warn the authorities of the cataclysm that will occur in the future? The answer is to find the time portal—the wormhole—that brought them to 2001. But the site has changed. It's no longer the place where they crossed the wormhole. Will they live out the balance of their lives beginning as teenagers?

"We've all wish we could go back to earlier times with the mind we have now. This Russell Moran book takes you there and it is a fun creative romp well worth reading. *A Reunion in Time* is highly recommend!" – Kindle Customer.

The President is Missing – Book Three of the Matt Blake series
http://amzn.to/2t9v7wu

While he was addressing the nation from a submerged nuclear submarine, President Blake's message is suddenly cut off. Anyone listening heard an explosion. The explosion was followed by floating debris five minutes later.

First Lady Dee Blake has doubts, which she shares with naval high command and the new president. She thinks the explosion and the debris were a ruse to make people think the sub was destroyed, and her husband with it.

Could the sub have been hijacked and the president kidnapped?

But who would commit such an act? What is its purpose?

Was it Russia, China, Iran, or a shadowy group of freelance terrorists?

The new president appoints Dee as his Chief of Staff, with explicit instructions to find the missing submarine—and President Matt Blake.

Her life, and the life of the nation, suddenly take a horrifying turn.

"Russ Moran wrote a true thriller, with a strong plot and even stronger characters. To think that there are good guys - Russian Naval Admirals, no less - made this book not only a solid who-done-it but also a strong 'why did they do it?' " – Unka Heshie

Robot Depot
http://amzn.to/2zXW7C2

Mike Bateman is a visionary businessman, the creator and CEO of the fabulously successful chain of stores, Robot Depot, a company dedicated to selling robots and Artificial Intelligence machines for a variety of uses.

The company is a darling of Wall Street and is the most popular destination for consumers and businesses looking for labor saving devices.

But the company caught the eye of ISIS, the terrorist Islamic State. They discover a great way to deliver bombs – using the products of Robot Depot to kill people.

Robot Depot changed from being a popular company to an object of fear because of the tampered products it sells. The terrorists use the company for "terror spectaculars," including the destruction of a skyscraper, a drone attack on Yankee Stadium, and the bombing of a children's sailing regatta.

Mike Bateman and the FBI are in a race to stop his products from becoming weapons, a race to stop the wanton killings. His wife and partner, Jenny, discovers the true meaning of terror one horrible summer day.

"Moran just got a new fan. This is the first book of Moran's that I've read, but I look forward to reading more of his work. I enjoyed this story, and found that Moran is not only a good writer, but he's a good storyteller as well. It's an interesting and creative story, mixing new technology and AI uses, with terrorism. It's a thriller that keeps the reader turning the page, and it's extremely captivating. I enjoyed the story and look forward to future works of his." – Amy's Bookshelf

A Climate of Doubt
https://amzn.to/2OSwcHR

Forget what you ever heard about climate change.

Forget your preconceived notions about reality itself.

Instantly, you are in a new world, a horrifying world, a world you don't understand.

On a hot summer day, Homeland Security Secretary, Rick Bellamy, and his wife Ellen, a famous TV talk show host, walked along the ocean front trying to escape the heat. Suddenly the temperature dropped from the high 90s to below freezing in a matter of minutes. It began to snow—*on July 16.*

The temperatures across the country and the world plummeted, creating winter in summer.

Bellamy and the rest of the government struggled to cope with the suddenly new climate, but to cope, they first had to find out what happened.

Scientists from academia blamed the weather on a sudden acceleration of climate change, but they were unable to explain a 60-degree temperature drop in a matter of minutes.

Two astronauts in an American space station realized that the sudden weather calamity coincided with a test of the 20 satellites that the space station controlled.

Attention focused on a huge American corporation that owned the space station and the satellites. Could there be a connection between the satellite tests and the radical drop in temperature?

As the deaths piled up and the world economy tilted toward disaster because of gigantic summer blizzards, Rick Bellamy and his team struggled to find answers before it was too late. Was it a sudden shift in climate change or did it have something to do with the satellites? The biggest question remained—was the catastrophe an accident, or was somebody controlling the weather? Was it terror?

Bundle up and get this page-turning thriller. You're in for a wild ride. The book was published in May of 2018. It's Book Four of the Matt Blake Series. Matt and Dee Blake take on their biggest challenge to date, along with our old friends, Rick and Ellen Bellamy.

"Mr. Moran does a masterful job of crafting an action-packed, suspenseful read about the devastating consequences of climate manipulation. The diabolical mastermind behind the caper is a dictator of the worst kind—a man without conscience who cares only for power. Through the magic of Mr. Moran's digital pen, the men and woman in white hats are three-dimensional and vividly real. While this is a work of fiction, it's plausible fiction. We can easily relate to the horrific consequences of such an act of terrorism as so capably portrayed in Mr. Moran's prose." – Colorado Avid Reader

***The Maltese Incident – A Story of Time Travel* (Book One of the Harry and Meg Series), the prequel to *The Violent Sea*.**
https://amzn.to/2RclZCT

You're on a beautiful cruise ship.

The April sky is full of stars.

Suddenly, the ship rumbles, and instantly the stars disappear.

"What the hell was that?" Captain Fenton yelled.

"Beats me, captain. I've never seen anything like it," the first officer said.

They would soon discover that the ship, *The Maltese*, had just traveled through time—millions of years to the past.

The captain, Harry Fenton, a highly decorated naval war hero, realizes the greatest battle of his life lay ahead of him.

Captain Harry, a widow, falls in love with a beautiful passenger, Meg Johnson, an executive with the company that owns the ship.

After a whirlwind romance, they marry—in the ship's ballroom—100 million years in the past.

Captain Harry convinces the passengers and crew that they must move ashore to a tropical island because the ship is running out of fuel and supplies. He organizes a group to go ashore and inspect the island.

An ancient forest inhabited by dinosaurs awaits them.

Meg wants to go with them. Harry, fearing for her safety, tries to convince her to stay on the ship.

Meg demonstrates that she is proficient with a gun by taking apart a rifle and reassembling it—in 15 seconds. Harry marvels that he's never seen such an expert gun handler—or accurate shooter. So, AR-15 in hand, Meg joins the inspection party. Charging dinosaurs are no match for Meg Fenton's firepower.

Will the 1,000 souls ever make it back to the time they came from, or will they remain stranded in the distant past?

A scientist aboard theorizes that, to return to their present time, they need to go back to the time portal, or wormhole, that brought them to the past.

But the ship doesn't have enough fuel for the journey.

Realizing that their lives have hit the reset button, the crew and passengers construct a community in the forest–Malta Town.

Under Harry and Meg's leadership, they create a court system, a legislature, and all the elements of a small budding democracy. Meg figures out a way to harness hydroelectric power from a nearby waterfall. Everybody thinks of Harry and Meg as the heart and soul of Malta Town. They begin their new lives—among the dinosaurs.

The Maltese Incident is a riveting tale of time travel, love, courage, and horror.

Get this page turner now and prepare for the ride of your life.

"As with Moran's work, he continues to be a great storyteller. I recommend reading this from title to end. It's well written, and filled with intensity and levity." – Amy's Bookshelf

The Violent Sea – A Story of Time TravelBook Two of the Harry and Meg Series, the sequel to **The Maltese Incident.**
https://amzn.to/2AT5ypI

The Violent Sea is a novel of war, time travel, military history, the second in the Harry and Meg Series. It's also a sweet romance between Harry and his wife, Meg.

Rear Admiral Harry Fenton has done it again. He's traveled through time to a different era. He finds himself, with a serious head injury from a fall, at Pearl Harbor Base Hospital on May 16, 1942, three weeks before the Battle of Midway. His wife and aide, Lieutenant Meg Fenton, is worried sick, and waits for him—in 2018.

Admiral Harry is the commanding officer of Carrier Strike Group 14 in 2018, but the people in 1942 think he's a busted-up hallucinating sailor who imagines himself an admiral.

Admiral Raymond Spruance is commanding officer of Carrier Task Force 16. After hearing about Harry's time travel stories, Spruance orders him brought to his flagship, the *USS Enterprise*. After Harry tells him about his time travel experiences, Spruance is convinced the man is insane.

But after speaking to him at length, Spruance is amazed at Harry's knowledge of naval tactics and strategy. He calls Harry's bluff and orders him to stay aboard the *Enterprise* for her upcoming engagement at the Battle of Midway.

By the end of the battle, Spruance is convinced Harry is an admiral, and thinks of him as a friend.

Now Harry needs to figure out how to travel back to 2018, to his carrier command, but most importantly, to the love of his life, Lieutenant Meg.

After Harry returns to the present, the Fentons are deployed on Harry's flagship, the *USS Gerald R. Ford*. The ship encounters another wormhole, this one in the ocean. They are transported to 1944 and participate in the Battle of Leyte Gulf.

The book took me 10 months to write. It went through 20 drafts and three rounds with my editors. I did copious research for the book to ensure its historical accuracy. If you enjoy the genre of time travel, I think you will love this book. I got to know my two main characters in the prequel, *The Maltese Incident.* Harry and Meg are deeply in love but enjoy constant banter and wisecracks. One of my favorite characters, Admiral Ashley Patterson of *The Gray Ship,* makes an important cameo appearance in *The Violent Sea.*

"What a great book. You will love this book. Time travel telling at its best. At the end you will believe it is possible. Russell Moran has crafted a great continuation from *The Maltese Incident* his character development has continued from the first book thru out this book and possibly beyond. His writing is so detail oriented you will find yourself believing that time travel is not only real but possible. This book was given to me as a gift but it turned out to be one of the greatest gifts I have ever received. You will find that your investment of money and time reading this book to be a great investment. Time and money both well spent." – Mike the Mailman

A Sea of Fear – **A Novel of Time Travel - Book 3 of The Harry and Meg Series.**
https://amzn.to/2GERuSx

You're Five-Star Admiral Harry Fenton, whom President Blake calls the greatest fighting admiral in American history.

Along with your Navy Commander wife, Meg, you lead your carrier strike group against the worst enemy the country has faced since World War II, a small nation that is intent on destroying the world's shipping industry. The seas of the world have become scenes of plunder, pillage, and mass murder.

The president has convinced you to come out of retirement and put an end to the looming crisis. He promotes you to Fleet Admiral, the highest-ranking officer since Admiral Chester Nimitz.

You and Meg were having a pleasant retirement, running a world-class resort that you bought in Rhode Island. But when the president pleads you to "Give 'em Hell, Harry," you know that you can't ignore his call to duty.

As people who have time traveled in the past, you come up with an idea to travel three years into the future. With President Blake's blessing, you and Meg lead a group of officers into the future. What you find is horrifying, an America taken over by a totalitarian dictator.

You return to the past and report your findings. President Blake, hearing your terrifying story, convinces you that you have an even bigger call to duty, the greatest challenge of your life. You take on the challenge for one reason—Meg will be at your side.

As in the first two books of the Harry and Meg Series, *The Maltese Incident* and *The Violent Sea, A Sea of Fear* is a sweet romance between two of literature's most exciting and likable characters, Harry and Meg Fenton.

A Sea of Fear is a story of war, politics, time travel, and love.

"This story is incredible. I felt like it was real-life and happening NOW! The way the political world is unfolding with the lies and innuendos, something like this could be possible. The main couple, husband and wife, Meg and Harry worked together to solve and help the nation climb onto its rock-solid feet. Surely this is the integrity that the United States government stands for. They had me in their corner wanting to see them win against the evil Antonio Martin. Read the story, it will enthrall and pull you in as it did me...Great ending." – Cristella

Leonardo Murphy – A Coming of Age Thriller
https://amzn.to/31vzC4S

You just launched a satellite into space without a rocket.

You invented a computer algorithm that writes novels.

You just entered Harvard University on a full scholarship after completing high school in two years.

Not bad for a 12-year-old kid.

Leonardo changed his name from William to Leonardo to honor his hero, Leonardo da Vinci. Young Leonardo Murphy has the second highest IQ ever recorded.

Leonardo, now 25, met a beautiful young woman named Janice, and fell madly in love. They married a year later.

Janice and Leonardo, who she calls "Lee," collaborate on various projects with the CIA and FBI.

But their intelligence activities put a target on their backs. They narrowly escape four assassination attempts.

Leonardo Murphy is a breathtakingly fast coming-of-age thriller about one of the most fascinating characters you will ever meet in literature. Instantly, you are shoulder to shoulder with the world's most amazing genius.

"Finally, a believable super hero comes to life! Peaks and valleys of horrific actions are neatly juxtaposed against comic relief. The humor, ranging between the poles of mild to downright hysterical, will surely tickle your funny bone. The frequent use of the protagonist's favorite word (26 matches found throughout), which I won't divulge, would ordinarily belabor one's prose, save when Leonardo employs the term. As a matter of fact, the story concludes with that very word, but rather endearingly. No, I did not ruin the ending for you folks. You'll see." – Robert Banfelder

The Pineaire Incident – Book 4 of the Harry and Meg Series
https://amzn.to/2VXQ2lp

One hundred gigantic fast submarines suddenly appear in the ocean.

President Harry Fenton and his First Lady, Meg are shocked by the event, as are all the leaders of the world.

Where are the submarines from? What do they want? What are their intentions?

Six Russian submarines attack one of the mystery subs. All six Russian subs are destroyed in two minutes.

President Fenton, along with Meg, reaches out to contact the leader of the strange fleet. They are amazed to discover that the subs are from another planet, Planet Pineaire.

But they're pleased to find out that the Pinearians came in peace, and bring with them an amazing gift, a new type of fuel that can revolutionize life on earth.

Get ready for an interplanetary thrill ride. *The Pinaire Incident* is Book 4 of the Harry and Meg series.

"Right at the beginning, we learn that 100 giant submarines are discovered with no idea how they could all suddenly appear. Being familiar with Harry & Meg, I immediately presumed they must have Time Traveled from some future time. Uh Oh, I almost gave away an important detail. You should already know that Harry and Meg are President and First Lady having recently defeated a small rogue nation that destroyed the Cruise Ship industry and nearly took over the world's

Shipping Industry. You might think peaceful times are ahead when abruptly, 100 of these 1,800 foot long submarines appear. Five Stars." – The Holey One

Puzzles Book 1 – A Detective Love Story
https://amzn.to/2MI6TEo

Veteran police detectives Bobbie Nelson and Bob Lawton are partnered. They're both concerned that they may not get along. They're both highly skilled and love their work—They love to solve puzzles. They soon learn that they don't just love their jobs, they love each other. *Puzzles* is an action-packed police thriller wrapped around a sweet romance.

Bobbie and Bob are two of the most exciting and likeable characters you will find in literature.

"This book should be kept out of the hands of crooks, criminals, terrorists, and any others planning to do evil. There are so many techniques utilized by skilled detectives that are revealed that this book could be used as a training guide by the Bad Guys. Even so, the reality is that fundamental police work is what solves most crimes. Gathering and evaluating massive amounts of data and looking for patterns or repeating details is what our two main characters excel at." – The Holey One

"Russell Moran has done it again with Puzzles: A Detective Love Story. Each case builds upon earlier ones, with the BBs fine-tuning their puzzle-solving techniques to such a degree it's not long before the FBI and CIA reach out them to piece together more complicated scenarios impacting on society. Russell has created an easy-to-read and fast-paced story, which will keep you turning the pages late into the evening to find out what happens next. I can't wait for the next book in the series!" – R. J. Krzak

About the Author

In addition to the 19 novels discussed above, I also published five nonfiction books: *Justice in America: How it Works—How it Fails; The APT Principle: The Business Plan That You Carry in Your Head; Boating Basics: The Boattalk Book of Boating Tips; If You're Injured: A Consumer Guide to Personal Injury Law; How to Create More Time.* My latest nonfiction book is *The Novel - A Writer's Guide - Discover the Joy of Writing Fiction* published in November 2018.

I'm a lawyer and a veteran of the United States Navy I live on Long Island, New York, with my wife and editor, Lynda, a Shih-Tzu named Sammie, and a Golden Retriever named Maggie.

A Personal Request

I hope you enjoyed reading *Puzzles Book 2* as much as I enjoyed writing it. Bob and Bobbie are now two of my favorite characters. I think of them as old friends. You will be seeing more of them in future books.

Please consider leaving a brief review on amazon.com. Book reviews are the lifeblood of an author.

www.ingramcontent.com/pod-product-compliance
Lightning Source LLC
Chambersburg PA
CBHW071323250626
47159CB00004B/1442